Cuckoos on the Mersey. The Death of All Hope

Conrad Jones

A Child Protection Team Novel

The Detective Alec Ramsay Series
The Child Taker
Slow Burn
Criminally Insane
Frozen Betrayal
Concrete Evidence
Desolate Sands
Three
The Inspector Braddick Books (follows on from Ramsay)
Brick
Shadows
Guilty
Deliver us from Evil
The Anglesey Murders (runs alongside Braddick)
Unholy Island
A Visit from the Devil
Nearly Dead
A Child from the Devil
Dark Angel
What Happened to Rachel?
Good, Bad and Pure Evil
Circus of Nightmares
Unravelling
A Disturbing Thing Happened Today
Soft Target Series (features Tank from The Child Taker)
Soft Target
Tank
Jerusalem
18th Brigade
Blister
The Journey Series
The Journey
The Journey Back
The Journey Home
The Magic Dragons of Anglesey
The Rock Goblins
The Pirate's Treasure
Cuckoos on the Mersey
My name was Leo
The death of all Hope

Red Dragon Publishing LTD

ISBN: 978-1-7394066-4-6

Cuckoos on the Mersey 2

Dedication

I'm dedicating this series to my partner and the other amazing people who work in child protection.

Cuckoos is a new series inspired by the work that the child protection teams across the country carry out, seven days a week. The work that the child protection teams do is nothing short of incredible, but we often only hear about the mistakes that are made. They are a forgotten emergency service, up there with ambulance, fire and police. When they are called upon, they respond with professionalism and urgency to match any other service.

The children they save will go on to have children of their own and their legacy will echo through time for generations to come. Future generations will have children of their own because of what they did yesterday, today, and will do tomorrow.

You are heroes in our midst, each and every one of you.

Glossary of terms
CE Child Exploitation
PR Parental Responsibility
DV Domestic Violence
WP Witness Protection
PVPU Protecting Vulnerable Persons Unit
C and F Child and Family report.
EDD expected delivery date.
Strat. Strategy planning meeting

Chapter 1. Sam

SAM WATCHED THE COFFIN being lowered, to the sound of David Bowie's Heroes, Angela's favourite song of all time. She was David Bowie's biggest fan. There were only a handful of people in the crematorium; Angela didn't have any family and hardly any friends. He recognised her social workers and their manager, Jo Lilly. It was good of them to come and pay their respects, even if she called them witches. Angela was a troubled soul but meant no harm and they liked her despite her issues. She was taken from this planet far too early.

A tear ran down his cheek as her coffin disappeared from view, and it hit home that his best friend, the love of his life, was gone. That was too final, and he felt overwhelmed. The tears poured and his body was wracked with sobs. His vision was blurred, and breathing normally was difficult. He was taking short breaths and holding it too long. His hands began to shake, and he put them between his knees and squeezed. It took long minutes to gain control of himself. When he sat up, he caught Jo Lilly looking at him and she smiled and nodded as if to say, it's okay to cry. His breathing was calming when the curtains closed, and the doors opened. It was clear that their time in this place was spent. Thank you, good luck, goodbye and get out.

Next please.

The mourners began to file out of the door opposite the one they had entered, and another group of mourners was already waiting to go inside, coffin lifted and ready. It was like a well-oiled machine, gobbling up the dead, never tiring, never taking a day off or slowing down. Coffin after coffin were carried in and lowered into the bowels of the crematorium to face the flames.

Ashes to ashes, dust to dust.

He couldn't wait to get out of there. It was a place of permanent grief, where people spoke in whispers and the atmosphere was hushed and oppressive. The sadness was pervasive and lingered on the air and he felt like it was choking him. He made his way towards the door as quickly as he could without breaking into a run. The cold air hit him before he was at the door, but it was a relief.

Outside, the sky was slate grey, and the rain was bouncing off the tarmac. It did nothing to brighten his mood. He ran towards his car, which was parked at the far side of a horseshoe driveway, which led to and from the main road. The quickest way to where he was parked was to cut out the curve by running across the grass. He set off and within minutes, his shoes and socks were soaked. He avoided a flowerbed and stumbled on the grass. There was a second when he thought he might stay upright but he was wrong. Sam slipped on the wet grass and fell to his knees, muddying his hands and cheap suit pants. He swore as he stood, wiping the mud from his fingers on his trousers and decided that running across the grass wasn't a good idea, but it was too late to go back now.

When he reached his car, he opened the door and climbed inside. The windows misted immediately, and he turned on the engine and set the heater to clear the windscreen. Another hearse crawled onto the driveway with its passenger lying in a teak box. Sam's eyes were drawn to it despite not wanting to look. He shivered, cold and wet. A vehicle went by, and he thought it was the social workers. The other mourners had dispersed quickly. No one wanted to hang around and chat about Angela and reminisce about what a wonderful human being she had been. There would be no sharing of fond memories, funny anecdotes or toasting the dear departed; she would fade into obscurity quickly as the world carried on turning regardless of her departure. Here today, gone tomorrow but no one really notices. He turned on the radio and waited for the windscreen to clear.

The news was headlined by interest rates rising again and duty being increased on strong alcohol. Tax the poor again. The government was granting hundreds of licences for companies to drill for oil and gas in the North Sea, despite whining on about global warming. Fucking hypocrites, the lot of them. The windscreen finally cleared, and he checked the road was safe to pull out. He drove away and half listened to the doom and gloom on the radio until an appeal caught his attention. He turned up the volume. The police were appealing for anyone with information about the disappearance of Anthony Head from the Huyton area of Liverpool, to contact them, anonymously or not. The news reader said that Tony Head had told his wife that he was going to meet a friend in the Bluebell pub for a pint but never arrived and hadn't been seen since. The police and his family were concerned about his whereabouts and well-being. Sam didn't know for sure that he'd been murdered but the fact that he never went home was a strong indication that he was dead.

Sam felt a shiver run down his spine, not from the cold this time, but from fear and guilt. Fear that the police would find his body and investigate his murder and guilt that he'd been involved in taking a husband and father away from his family, even if he was a rapist.

His family weren't responsible for his sins, that was on him alone. Sam had seen his wife, Sandra, several times, putting up missing posters in the village. She looked like she'd been crying for weeks, and her cheeks were hollow and drawn as if she wasn't eating. There were posts daily on social media, increasingly desperate as time ticked by. He wanted to put her out of her misery and tell her to move on but how could he? Sam knew her husband wasn't coming home, and why but she didn't, and it was haunting him. At the moment, Anthony Head was a missing person. Only Sam and his kidnappers knew different.

The drive home was dreary, raining constantly. Sam turned onto the estate and nearly flattened a youngster on a mountain bike, who was riding on the wrong side of the road. He was pedalling furiously, head down, teeth bared. Sam swerved to avoid him and spotted three of the local scrotes riding electric scooters at full pelt behind him, all dressed in uniform black tracksuits. They appeared to be chasing the cyclist. It explained why he was hurtling down the wrong side of the road. He sounded his horn, warning the scooter-scrotes not to come too close but they just whizzed by, flicking the finger. They were fearless and roamed the streets in packs, terrorising anyone not in their gang.

Sam drove on without further incident and parked outside his flat. He glanced towards Angela's house and his heart sank. The housing association had been in and emptied it. They had painted everywhere white, removed the rubbish from the gardens and cut the lawns, ready for the next family to move in. She was gone and erased from her home in just a few weeks. Movement to his left caught his eye and he glanced at the Head residence. Sandra Head was standing in the front window staring at the world outside, waiting for her husband to return home. Sam felt sick.

He locked his car and walked to his building's entrance door. It had been left open again, which infuriated Sam. Some of the residents didn't give a shit about security. He stepped into the hallway and instantly smelled weed. It was the powerful stuff, probably skunk. It had a very distinctive odour which lingered for hours. He hated the brain-numbing shit and the deadheads who smoked it. No one in his block smoked in the communal areas, especially not weed. The residents were mostly a decent bunch now. All the bad eggs had been evicted, jailed, or were dead. He looked around the hallway.

Les's front door was open, and he was dead, so it didn't take Sherlock to explain where the stink was coming from. No one had moved into the flat yet, not officially anyway. The handle was hanging loose, so it had been forced. Sam could hear music from inside and he knew the empty flat had been cuckooed. He thought about knocking on the door and asking them to fuck off, but it wasn't worth becoming a target. He shut the front door and crept to the stairs as quietly as he could. It was his home, and he shouldn't be creeping around, but he didn't want to provoke confrontation with whoever had broken in. Whoever they were, they were not nice people. He reached his flat and let himself inside, leaning against the door. The lock clicked and he bolted it, feeling safer that way. He could hear the bassline of the music, boom, boom, boom. It would do his head in, but it wouldn't be forever. They weren't his new neighbours; they were cuckoos, and they would fly the nest when the police arrived. He walked to his front window and looked across the road. Sandra Head was still standing in her window, still watching, still waiting, and still suffering.

Chapter 2. Boothy

A nd if you have a minute, why don't we go, talk about it somewhere only we know...

GARY BOOTH WAS THE youngest of Barry Maddern's inner circle and the only one not in prison or dead. The members of the lower echelons of the outfit were still at large and most of them were rallying to Boothy. The death of Mad Maddern had triggered violent infighting between the remaining lieutenants who were vying for the top spot. It had also triggered brutal incursions into their postcodes by rival outfits, trying to mop up his gang's territory. Several of their street dealers had been robbed, badly beaten and stabbed. There was blood in the water and the sharks were circling, looking to feed on the debris. It was an unsettled and dangerous time and old feuds were being rekindled, sparking gang wars across the Northwest.

At just twenty-four, Boothy wasn't deemed a serious long-term threat by their rivals, and that meant they had massively underestimated him. He had been training in MMA since a young age and had won all his fights in the octagon before a knee injury ended his career. With no weight divisions or blood tests to worry about anymore, he hit the steroids at nineteen and twelve months later, was a monster. Being twenty-four was irrelevant. He wasn't looking to step into Barry Maddern's shoes, he was already wearing bigger shoes of his own.

Before Leo Tompkins had dropped the atomic bomb on the Maddern gang, Boothy had been tasked with supplying the smaller dealers and young gangs across the city and there were dozens of them; it was his job to keep everyone in line and stamp out insurrection when it raised its head. They were mostly teenagers on bikes, selling ket, speed and cocaine to other teenagers but they were sixty percent of the business. His physical size and reputation as a fighter had stood him in good stead and the youngsters looked up to him. Boothy was an icon to the young criminals on Merseyside. Without trying to, he had built up a rapport, networking with the younger criminals over years, and the turf war that was raging now had little interest to them. The young gangs were operating on a different level and as long as they could make a few quid, they were happy. The lower level of the criminal underworld was stable.

As far as the other main players in the city were concerned, Boothy had operated under the radar for years and hadn't made any enemies, unlike the rest of Maddern's outfit. His rise to the top went unnoticed and that allowed him to organise and regroup in relative safety. Boothy was fully aware of where Maddern kept his supplies of drugs and weapons. Leo had given the police some of the less significant stocks of gear and caches of firearms, but he was too far down the pecking order to have known where all of them were. Boothy knew where everything was and was gathering whatever he could and relocating it before anyone else turned into a grass.

He was on his way to Warrington to a storage facility, part of his consolidating the Maddern remnants. He was continuing the business with himself at the helm and wasn't too concerned about who wasn't happy with that. They pulled off the M62 and drove towards the Gemini retail park.

'We're here,' Kirk said, bringing the Jeep to a halt in a disabled parking bay outside Storage World. Kirk was black and had worked for the Madderns since before Boothy was born. His hair and beard were more grey than dark, but his shoulders were still wider than his waist and there was concussive power in each hand. He was a seasoned gangster and with his old boss dead, had pledged his loyalty behind Boothy because he knew he would live longer that way. 'Are you sure this is the right place? I've never been here before,' he asked. 'I'm sure I haven't, although my memory isn't what it used to be.'

'I'm sure it's the right place. No one has been here except Barry and Uncle Ged,' Boothy said. Ged Tickle was married to Boothy's aunt and had been arrested and remanded in jail awaiting trial for conspiracy to supply. 'This one was kept between them, but Uncle Ged told me about it when I visited him at Risley last week, so I need to check it out,' Boothy lied. He had found a series of bank transfers to this storage facility but when he'd asked his uncle if there were any more stashes that he didn't know about, Ged had lied about this one. The fact he had failed to mention Storage World meant there was something in there that he didn't want Boothy to find. He went to his flat and searched for anything related to the facility and found an access card with the brand printed on it.

'Do you want me to come with you to carry the gear?' Kirk asked. 'I could do with stretching my legs.'

'No need,' Boothy said, opening the door. 'I want to double check what's in here and make a note of it in my head. No one knows about this stash, so it can stay here for now.'

He climbed out and closed the door, jogging through the rain to the reception. The security guard was wearing a pristine blue uniform and cap. He was sitting behind a plastic screen watching football on a small device. Behind him was a young man wearing a short-sleeved shirt and tie. His badge said he was the Site Manager, and his name was Rupert Stokes. Boothy smiled and showed the access card that he had found. The guard took it and scanned it. The manger saw the details on the screen and handed the card back to Boothy without asking for identification, which meant money had changed hands somewhere.

'Your unit is on the second floor, turn left out of the lift, it's the fourth unit on the right,' he said, pointing to the lift. 'Are you removing anything because the trolleys are over there?'

'I don't think so. Not this time,' Boothy said, shaking his head. 'Thanks for your help.'

'No problem,' the manager said. 'If you change your plans, just take one of the trolleys and leave it on the car park when you're finished.'

'Cheers, I will. Thank you.'

Boothy walked to the lift and pressed the button for the second floor. The facility was relatively new and spotless. There wasn't any sign of damage or deterioration. He could smell pine disinfectant in the air. The lift door opened, and he walked along the corridor to the unit. There was nobody else around when he opened the door and stepped inside. The lights came on, triggered by a sensor. It was a small unit and empty apart from a freezer and an aluminium storage trunk, which was in the centre of the floorspace. There were two brass clasps and two padlocks. Boothy took a bunch of keys from his pocket and opened one of the locks and a clasp, then opened the other side. He paused for a second before opening the lid.

Inside were bundles of ten-pound notes, banded and vacuum packed. He reached inside and counted the packets. Boothy figured there was fifty thousand in each packet and there were four stacks of ten. Two million. This was Uncle Ged's escape money if he had the chance to skip bail or his pension for when he got out of prison. No wonder he wanted to keep it secret. He must have been on the take from Maddern for years.

Boothy locked the trunk and turned his attention to the freezer. It was plugged into the mains and padlocked. He found the key on the third attempt and opened the lock. The motor hummed, almost silently. He wasn't anticipating the freezer to be stocked full of chicken breasts and bags of peas. He lifted the lid. Boothy didn't recognise him.

Anthony Head was squashed inside, his limbs removed and wrapped in clingfilm, frozen solid. The torso was in the centre, his head removed, and placed on his chest, vacuum packed in cellophane. His eyes were open and rolled backwards and his mouth was open wide, in a silent scream. He could make out the stump of a hand in another package, the fingers removed. Whoever it was, he had died slowly and in agony.

Uncle Ged had not told him about the unit for good reason. The contents could get him locked away for life but the fact he hadn't asked him to deal with the contents, meant he didn't trust him and that was a huge problem. Trust was everything. Without trust, the relationship was a sham, and he couldn't risk working with anyone he didn't trust.

Boothy had no idea who the man in the freezer was and it didn't matter. Uncle Ged was looking at a long prison sentence anyway and didn't want murder added to it. Boothy took out his mobile and snapped three photographs of the contents. He closed the lid and padlocked the freezer before heading back downstairs in the lift. When the doors opened, he stepped out and headed to the trolleys. The guard looked up from his device, his manager gone now.

'I'm going to take something out,' Boothy said. 'Can I use one of these?'

'Of course,' the guard said, nodding. 'Do you need a hand?'

'No thanks,' Boothy said. 'I can manage.'

He went back to the unit and opened the door. The light flickered on. He lifted the trunk onto the trolley as if it was empty and then wheeled it out of the unit, locking the door behind him. The trolley had a squeaky wheel, which was annoying him, but he dragged it through the reception to the Jeep without any problems. Kirk jumped out of the driver's seat and opened the boot.

'I thought you were leaving it here?' Kirk said. 'Had a change of mind?'

'It's not what I thought it was,' Boothy said, lifting the trunk into the boot.

'What's in it?' Kirk asked, frowning.

'An opportunity, Kirk,' Boothy said. 'And my old dad always said, never miss an opportunity.'

'I'll try not to,' Kirk said, smiling. 'Where are we going with the opportunity?'

'I want to stash it somewhere only we know,' Boothy said.

'In the Bootle lockup?' Kirk suggested.

'No. Somewhere where it will never be found,' Boothy said.

Chapter 3. The Norris Home

W hen I can't sleep at night, looking out at the white world and the Moon, I feel a soft exchange taking place...

HOPE NORRIS WAS TWELVE years old going on twenty. She was dressing her two sisters and younger brother for school as their mother was still in bed, suffering from whatever she had drunk the night before. Paige and Pru were ten-year-old twins and Jacob was eight. They were chattering and laughing as they washed, dressed and then went downstairs for breakfast. Their mother was emotionally and physically absent most of the time. Hope looked after her siblings. It was just another day in the Norris household.

Hope put the last four pieces of bread into the toaster and grabbed four small plates from the cupboard. She opened the fridge and took out the milk and butter. There was only a shrivelled onion and some cheese which had gone white and crusty left in there. She tutted and made a note that food supplies were zero.

'Get some glasses for the milk,' she said to Paige. Paige took four glasses from the drainer and filled them with milk. 'Here, Jacob. Drink your milk. It will make you big and strong.'

'I am going to drink it all,' Jacob said, slurping from the glass. He licked at the residue on his top lip. 'Milk makes you grow. I'm nearly as tall as you are.'

'You are,' Hope said. 'But if you don't start eating your vegetables, you'll shrink.'

'You've made that up,' Jacob said, smiling. 'I don't believe that. No one shrinks.'

'It's true,' Hope said. 'Milk makes you grow, carrots help you to see in the dark, fish makes you brainy and an apple a day keeps the doctor away, runner beans make you run faster and vegetables stop you shrinking.'

'No,' Jacob objected, shaking his head. 'You made up the last bit.' He thought about it. 'Can we have runner beans for tea?'

'Yes. Ask mum to get some when she goes shopping.'

'I'm not sure I believe you that I can shrink,' Jacob said, smiling.

'It's all true,' Hope said.

'It is,' Paige agreed. 'I've heard it a million times.'

'Yes, I have heard it before but where does it say that not eating vegetables makes you shrink?' Jacob said.

'In the Bible,' Hope said, trying not to laugh. She kept her face straight.

'In the Bible?' Jacob said, frowning.

'It's true,' Paige agreed. 'And the Lord said, thou must eat your veggies.'

Jacob looked doubtful but didn't know enough about the Bible to argue. He smirked and sipped his milk.

'You lot are so noisy. We were trying to have a lie in.' The voice of David Isle made them all look up. He was their mother's boyfriend and unpopular to say the least. She had been with a few boyfriends, who had moved in but none of them lasted more than a few weeks.

'Sorry about that but some of us can't lie in bed all day. We have to get up and go to school,' Hope said. She disliked him with a passion. He was a letch. She had seen the way he looked at her and he gave her the creeps.

'Is there any milk left?' David asked, opening the fridge. 'We want a cup of tea.'

'Sorry. We've just used the last of it,' Hope said, downing her milk. Her sisters followed suit. 'Drink up, Jacob.' Jacob swallowed his in two gulps. Hope buttered the toast and handed her siblings a piece each. 'That's the last of the bread too. Tell mum not to worry, I've got the kids ready for school and we need a shop if she can be bothered getting out of bed today.'

'Don't talk about your mother like that.'

'There's nothing in the fridge or the cupboards for tea tonight,' Hope said. 'I'm just saying that we need a shop, that's all. They'll be hungry when they get home from school.'

'That's because you greedy little bastards eat her out of house and home,' David said, opening the fridge. 'You're like a swarm of locusts. I can't believe you haven't left enough milk for us to have a brew. Selfish little brats. All you do is take, take, take. Fucking brats.'

'Fuck off, David,' Hope said, grabbing the coats and bags from the coat hooks. 'And don't call us brats. You're not our dad and when I tell my dad what you've just said, he'll come and batter you.'

'Not in this lifetime or the next,' David said, frowning. The dislike of Hope was clearly etched into his face. 'He's a dickhead and unless you hadn't noticed, he's being bummed in the showers at Walton prison. He's not coming anywhere near this house for at least three years.'

'I'm going to tell him what you said anyway. His friends are well hard and they're not in jail. They'll come here and batter you,' Hope said.

'Will they really?' David sneered.

'Yes. Just you wait and see.'

'Ooh!' David bit his fingertips. 'I'm so scared, I can't stop shaking.' He snorted. 'Stupid little bitch,' he muttered. 'Go to school before I lose my temper and give you what you deserve.'

'And what do I deserve, David?' Hope snapped.

'A fucking good hiding.' David pointed his finger. 'Your mum is too soft on you brats but if you keep pushing me, young lady, you'll see a side of me that you won't like.'

'We don't like any side of you,' Hope said. 'We think you're a prick.'

'You have a smart mouth on you. I'd go to school if I was you.'

Hope could see the venom in his eyes and despite all her bluster, she was scared of David. She knew she was pushing the limits and put on her coat. The siblings filed out of the back door in silence. Jacob glared at David, protecting his big sister. David glared back. They walked down the path to the pavement.

'I hate him,' Jacob said. 'He's a wanker.'

'Don't you use that word in school,' Hope said, smiling. 'You'll get into trouble.'

'When I grow up, I'm going to batter him,' Jacob said.

'He won't be around when you grow up,' Hope said, ruffling his hair. 'He'll be long gone by then.'

'Jacob is right though. He is a wanker though,' Paige said, chuckling.

They began walking towards school and a lorry drove by, deafening them. Jacob put his fingers in his ears. Across the road, three of the older lads from school were sitting on a wall smoking. They nodded hello and Hope returned the gesture. She didn't like them. They smoked weed and inhaled laughing gas in the park. One of them was selling stuff at school. He was a bully but always said hello to Hope. She figured it was better to have the bullies onside.

'He is a wanker,' Jacob agreed. 'I don't know why mum is with him.'

'We all know he's a wanker,' Hope began. 'But we need to be careful what we say when he's around...aaah!' She screamed. Hope grabbed her face and fell to the floor, her eyes wide with fear and pain. Blood ran between her fingers.

'What happened?' Paige shouted. 'Hope, what happened.'

Hope shook her head, confused.

'She's bleeding,' Jacob said, panicking.

'We need someone to call an ambulance. Don't worry, Hope,' Pru said, stroking Hope's hair. 'Go and get help.'

'Okay,' Paige said, looking around. 'I'll go and tell mum.'

'What happened to Hope?' the next-door neighbour, Doreen, shouted from her front door. 'I saw her fall down. What happened to her?'

'We don't know,' Paige shouted. 'Her face is bleeding.'

Doreen came running down the path. She was a middle-aged lady with her hair in a bob, still wearing her dressing gown. 'Is she alright?'

'She's bleeding,' Jacob said. 'She just screamed and fell down on the floor.'

'Let me see where the blood is coming from,' Doreen said, kneeling down. 'I know you're scared, Hope but I need to see where the blood is coming from. I'm going to move your hand, Hope. Let me see what's going on, lovely.'

She moved her fingers and saw a dark hole in Hope's temple. The edges were perfectly circular. There was a lead pellet buried in the wound. Blood pumped from the wound with every heartbeat.

'She's been shot. That's a pellet,' Doreen said.

'A pellet?' Jacob said. 'Like from a gun?'

'An airgun. Someone has shot her with an air rifle.' Doreen took out her phone and dialled 999. 'Police and ambulance, please,' she said. 'A twelve-year-old girl has been shot in the face with a pellet gun. It's lodged in her temple and she's bleeding.' Doreen gave the address and went through to the police. They were alerted that a firearm had been used.

'Is she going to die?' Jacob asked, panicking. 'Why is the ambulance not here yet? Will she die?'

'No lovely,' Doreen said. 'We'll stop the bleeding, and the ambulance will be here soon.'

'Why would anyone shoot at Hope?' Paige asked, crying. She turned full circle, looking for where the shot could have been fired from.

'I don't know, lovely,' Doreen said, shaking her head. 'But the police will find out who did it and they'll lock them up.'

'Some of my friends' older brothers have air rifles,' Jacob said. 'But they don't shoot at people with them.'

'No darling,' Doreen said. 'They shouldn't do that.' She pointed at the Norris house. 'Go and tell your mum what has happened. The police will want to speak to all of you.'

Chapter 4. Jo Lilly

Hush, can you hear the trees so far away, hush can you feel the breeze of another day?

JO LILLY WAS AT HER desk in Huyton, reading a raft of parenting assessments, which had been emailed that day and were due to be submitted the next day. Her Head of Service, Hayley Banks, was heading in her direction, a concerned look on her face. Jo turned to face her and put down her cup of tea.

'Morning Hayley,' Jo said, sitting up straight as if the headmistress had walked into the classroom. 'You look like you're on a mission, what's up?'

'We have supervision booked in for this afternoon,' Hayley said. She put her glasses on the end of her nose and looked over them, gesturing to Jo's screen. 'But I'm aware that you need to get those assessments in today. How are you getting on with them?'

'To be honest, they're a crock of shit,' Jo said, not beating around the bush. 'It's last-minute dot com again and I'm getting a bit sick of chasing deadlines when the team is working flat out just to get things done. We have to work smarter, to be fair. We need to move the submission deadline so that we have time to read and return highlighted copies of them to the social workers with recommendations attached without the panic. Then they can work on them and get them submitted with time to spare.'

'It's not rocket science and they're professional people with deadlines to meet. They all managed to earn their degrees, which meant they had to write and submit work on deadlines, so what's changed?'

'Pressure,' Jo said. 'We're creaking under the strain at the moment; something always gives when the pressure is turned up.'

'Pressure is always going to be there. The process is fine, it's their time management that is flawed. They need to be more organised. Why are they leaving things until the last minute?' Hayley said, shrugging.

'The team is usually spot on, but they're snowed under at the moment,' Jo said. 'We've got a couple of family support workers off, so my social workers are covering family contacts, which is a total waste of their time. It's eating into their daily routines, and they're racking up toil, working extra hours, so admin gets pushed to the back of the queue.'

'We're all busy, so that's no excuse. The assessments can't be rushed. It defeats the object. What's the quality like?' Hayley asked.

'I do wonder if my laptop is the only one with a spelling and grammar checker installed or do you think some people can't see red lines?' Jo said, smiling.

'I have often wondered the same thing. I have nightmares where all I can say is, 'spellcheck the effing document for heaven's sake',' Hayley said. 'Anyway, enough about parenting assessments. How is Lenny?'

'He's back to the gym and work is going well. He's selling cars and most of them don't bounce back,' Jo said, nodding. She pushed her long brown hair behind her ears. 'Gym and cars are his favourite things apart from me, of course. He won't talk about what happened though. He says he's coping in his own way.'

'How is he coping with it, really?' Hayley asked, cocking her head. Her expression was one of concern.

'A bit shit really.' Jo sat back and picked up her tea. 'He pretends everything is normal, but it isn't. He is mega-cautious about everything, which isn't like him. Lenny has walked around like he's indestructible for most of his life, but now he sees danger in everything. I think it has made him feel vulnerable.'

'That's only natural,' Hayley said. 'He suffered a terrible trauma and nearly died. Dealing with it mentally won't be easy.'

'I know. I have my beady eye on him. On the bright side, he has a bullet wound, which not a lot of people have, and he says that when he was a boy, he always wanted a bullet wound or duelling scar on his cheek, so every cloud...'

'I think that's a man thing,' Hayley said. 'I once saw an advert online where you could buy a duelling scar on your cheek. The procedure was done by a surgeon at a clinic in Paris, and they offered lovely accommodation in the package with a view of the Eiffel Tower.'

'How romantic, Paris and a slashed cheek, so you can look like the Action Man toy you played with as a kid. The world has gone mad,' Jo said, shrugging. 'Anyway, he's back to his old self, buying shite wine and moaning about the price of everything.' Jo stopped and thought for a second. 'On a more serious note, the police have asked him to go into the station to look at some mugshots.'

'What?' Hayley asked, surprised. 'Have they arrested the men who attacked him?'

'They won't say but hinted as much,' Jo said. 'The call was a bit cryptic. He's worried they might be relying on his identification to arrest them or keep them inside. Apart from his attackers, he was the only one there, so...'

'He's the only witness. That would mean they would need him to testify in court,' Hayley said, nodding. 'I can understand why that would worry him. It would worry me. They are dangerous men with dangerous friends.'

'You're not making me feel any better about it,' Jo said, biting her lip. 'I feel like telling him to leave it be and walk away from it but he's a stubborn ass. I think he will see it through out of principle, but I've told him there are a lot of proud men in the cemetery.'

'Pride comes before the fall, don't they say?' Hayley said. 'What did he say to that?'

'He told me stop being melodramatic,' Jo said. 'So, I told him to bog off and boil his head.'

'Sorry to interrupt, Jo, have you got a minute, please?' Phil Molt asked from the next desk. 'There's been a serious incident at the Norris family home.'

'What's happened?' Jo asked.

'Hope Norris, the eldest girl, has been shot in the face with an air rifle,' Phil explained. 'They're taking her to Alder Hey Hospital now. She has a pellet lodged in her temple.'

'Was she shot inside their home?' Hayley asked.

'No. She was outside on the pavement. She was on the way to school with her siblings when she collapsed onto the floor,' Phil said. 'They didn't hear the shot because of the traffic.'

'And no one saw where the shot came from?' Jo asked.

'Apparently not,' Phil said. 'The police are knocking on doors.'

'When were you last there at the house?' Jo asked.

'Last Tuesday,' Phil said. 'They're still on a CP plan. It was with team five for twelve months and they stepped it down last year, but they were back on a plan three months later.'

'What happened to put them back on a plan?' Hayley asked.

'The kids were going to school hungry and the youngest was caught stealing sandwiches from the local petrol station.'

'That will do it,' Hayley said, shaking her head.

'Mum is not engaging, and her boyfriend is an obnoxious dick. The children don't like him one bit. They're good kids, highly motivated, attend school, and are polite and well behaved.' Phil paused. 'The adults are the problem in that house.'

'They usually are,' Hayley agreed.

'The police are at the house and they're requesting that I visit as soon as,' Phil said. 'The siblings aren't opening up. They want to talk to me.'

'That's interesting. Get yourself over there and call the hospital. We need a child protection medical done on Hope, put in a strategy meeting with the police to agree a section 47 assault and let me know what you find at the home,' Jo said. 'If she was on the street, that pellet could have come from anywhere. See what the police have to say and let me know.'

'Will do,' Phil said, grabbing his coat. 'Talk later.'

Chapter 5. Lenny

It's cold outside and the paint is peeling off my walls, there's a man outside, in a long coat, grey hat, smoking a cigarette...

LENNY PARKED UP THE F-type Jag on the Estuary Business Park, Speke, home to the Matrix Squad. The three-storey building was relatively new and housed the units who dealt with organised crime, county lines and serious crimes. The Matrix Vehicle Enforcement Team were stabled there too, working alongside the Regional Organised Crime Unit (ROCU), North Wales Police, Cheshire Police and the Lancashire Constabulary, all trying to stem the rising tide of drugs and OCGs.

A group of officers were talking at the front door, hardly noticing him as he walked in, but he felt them glance in his direction and his pulse rate increased. He wasn't a criminal and was there to help the police but felt nervous anyway, even though he had a good working relationship with them. As a car dealer, the police were always in touch, asking for information on vehicles and their previous owners. Once a car was marked as being part of a criminal operation, it was difficult to wipe it off.

The reception desk was busy, and he waited in line, explaining he had an appointment with DCI Dunn, which had been arranged by a detective constable by the name of Harris. He was told to take a seat and that the officer would be with him shortly. Lenny spotted a seat which wasn't occupied and had no one else near it and headed for it. The last thing he wanted was a conversation with a stranger about why he was here. This wasn't the time or the place for pointless chitchat. He sat down and took out his phone, checking his emails and messages. There were three enquiries about vehicles, which was good, but he couldn't concentrate on the details because he was nervous. The business was making good money since Covid but being shot and battered to a pulp had slowed things down. Lenny had been targeted because Jo had placed Barry Maddern's children into care. He had a couple of salesmen at his car lot, who stepped up and ran things while he was recovering, and they kept the business afloat. Second hand cars were at a premium and he was making the most of it. His thoughts went back to the attack and the bullet wound ached as if it knew what he was thinking. Psychosomatic pain, the doctor called it.

'Are you Leonard Ray?' a female voice asked.

'Yes. Call me Lenny. Only my mum called me Leonard and that was when I was in trouble.' He looked up at a young female with her blonde hair fastened into a ponytail; the scent of Opium Black arrived with her. She had high cheekbones and green eyes and looked too young to be a police officer. 'I have a meeting with DCI Chris Dunn. Is he ready to see me?'

'Unfortunately, he's been knocked down by a bus, I'm afraid, so I've come instead,' she said, frowning. Lenny looked shocked.

'Oh...' Lenny muttered.

'Only joking,' she said. 'I'm DCI Dunn. Christine Dunn but people call me Chrissie or Chris.'

'Hello Chrissie,' Lenny said, laughing. 'I put my big foot in it there, didn't I?'

'You did a little,' Chrissie said, smiling. 'Don't worry about it. The look on your face was worth it.'

'I bet it was. You had me there for a minute.'

'Everyone expects me to be a man for some reason,' Chrissie said.

'Apologies. I meant no offence.'

'None taken. Follow me,' Chrissie said, walking away. 'I have a room set up on the ground floor, so no stairs to navigate. I know you're recovering from a gunshot wound. How are you healing up?'

'I'm getting there,' Lenny said. 'I'm lucky the bullet hit my belt buckle, or I'd be feeding the worms. I get aches and pains around the bullet wound but I'll take that over the alternatives.'

'I feel your pain,' Chrissie said, half turning. She weaved her way through the chairs in the waiting area to a door which accessed the interior of the station and tapped in the access code. 'I was stabbed in the back six years ago during a raid on a crack house and the wound still bothers me. It doesn't like the cold and sometimes it feels like the blade is still inside. I know it isn't, but I still feel it to check.'

'I get that feeling too, as if something is still there,' Lenny said, nodding. 'Sometimes, I wake up and think it's bleeding but obviously it isn't. I suppose it's all part and parcel of the healing process. My doctor says I have PTSD, which is hard to get my head around. Sounds a bit dramatic to me.'

'PTSD comes in all shapes and sizes, and we just have to accept it's part of who we became following the trauma,' Chrissie said as they walked. 'Violence traumatises us. It changes us as people, and we just have to adapt.'

'Wow. I never thought of it like that,' Lenny said. 'I suppose it does change you.'

'The force sent me to see a counsellor as part of my return to work,' Chrissie said. 'They were her words, not mine. Far too deep for me to come up with.'

'I work for myself,' Lenny said. 'And I'm too tight to pay for therapy.'

Chrissie laughed. She was tall and slim, wearing a dark suit with pants. Her dark trainers were Mallet. Lenny followed her through a maze of corridors to a room with glass walls.

'We're in here,' Chrissie said. She stepped aside and let him pass. 'Take a seat over there. Make yourself comfortable. There's bottled water on the table for you or would you prefer a tea or coffee?'

'Water is fine.'

'Okay. Let me explain how this will work. We're going to put some faces up on the screen there,' she said, pointing. 'This is Yasmin.' Yasmin waved a hand and smiled. 'Yasmin is a computer geek.'

'Technician,' Yasmin corrected.

'Geek, same thing. She puts the line-ups together from our data bases, which saves me from doing it because we would be here all day otherwise.'

'Hello Yasmin,' Lenny said. Yasmin was Chinese and tiny. She looked about fourteen. 'Nice to meet you.'

'Nice to meet you too,' Yasmin said. 'Is this your first time here?'

'Yes. I try to avoid police stations. When I was growing up, the only people who went into one, went in through the back door and rarely came out,' Lenny said, smiling. 'And some of them didn't come out for a long time.' He joked. 'I came in through the front. So far, it's not as bad as I thought it was going to be.'

'Really?' Yasmin said, smiling. 'Only most people hate being in here, especially the ones who work here. At least you can leave after this. We have to stay to the end of our shift.'

'We'll see how I get on. I might change my mind in the meantime,' Lenny said. 'We'll soon see.'

'We'll do our best to make sure you don't change your mind,' Chrissie said. She folded her arms. 'Before we begin, I want to be clear about what you remember. I know it's a while ago now, but I want to know what you can remember about what your attackers looked like. Are the memories clear or hazy?'

'I can remember them like it was yesterday,' Lenny said. 'Their faces are engrained in my mind.'

'Good. Are you up for looking at some mug shots?' Chrissie asked. She leaned on a desk and put her hands in her pockets.

'Before I say yes or no, I need to know what the score is,' Lenny said.

'I'm not sure what you mean?' Chrissie said. Yasmin looked up from her laptop, suddenly interested in the hiccup. 'Are you undecided about identifying your attackers?'

'You want me to point out the men who attacked me, but I need to know if they are in jail or are they still out and about?' Lenny said.

'The truth is, we don't know,' Chrissie said, shrugging. 'We have the majority of Barry Maddern's outfit locked up, but we don't know if the men who attacked you are amongst them or not. Only you know that.'

'I see,' Lenny said. He sat back and thought about it. 'So, they might be in jail already, but they might not?'

'They might be,' Chrissie said. 'Only you know who they were. Hence, we want you to identify them.'

'That is a shame,' Lenny said. 'I was hoping you might have half a dozen witnesses to the shooting, and you wouldn't need me at all.'

'Unfortunately not. We monitor chat on social media and phones, but the gang members are not saying anything about anything, so we don't even have any gossip or speculation to go on. We're still trawling through mobile phone messages but so far, we have got nothing relating to you. We don't rule out anyone at this stage, but we can't rule anyone in either.' Lenny nodded and folded his arms. 'We know who Maddern's shooters were and they're inside, but we can't presume one of them shot you. You are our only hope at prosecuting someone for your attack.'

'Okay, I understand what you're saying to me. I'm the only one who can identify them,' Lenny said, nodding. He sighed. 'If I identify them and they're not inside, what then?'

'They would be arrested and charged with attempted murder,' Chrissie said, making eye contact for a second too long. He could see anxiety in her eyes.

'Okay, let's be honest with each other,' Lenny said. 'We both know it doesn't work like that.'

'I'm being as honest as I can,' Chrissie said, shaking her head. 'What are you not comfortable with?'

'Cards on the table. If they are still on the outside, they'll be nervous about all the arrests. They'll be waiting for a tap on the shoulder or a knock on the door and I'm sure they will have sorted out alibis by now. They have had plenty of time to cover their tracks,' Lenny said. Chrissie nodded but didn't speak. 'I've been around criminals all my working life and I know how it works. If you arrest them and they have an alibi, they walk and I'm the only one who can put them away, so they will want to shut me up for good.' Lenny shrugged. 'I don't fancy being shot again and I'm not putting my missus in danger too.'

'I get that, Lenny, but what you're forgetting is that they know you saw their faces,' Chrissie said. 'They left you for dead because they thought you were dead. But you survived the attack and can identify them because they didn't bank on you living.'

'What are you saying?' Lenny asked, frowning. 'I don't like the sound of that.'

'There's a target on your back whether you pick them out today or not,' Chrissie said, shrugging. 'Your best bet is to make sure they're inside for the next twenty years and then you're not looking over your shoulder.'

'Fucking hell,' Lenny mumbled. 'I never thought of it like that. If they were going to take me out of the game, wouldn't they have done it by now?'

'Not necessarily. They may be inside, or they might be lying low,' Chrissie said. 'We know several associates of Maddern went to

Thailand on extended visas, another is in Benidorm and a couple went to the USA. I could speculate until the cows come home but until you point out who they were, that's all it is, pure speculation.'

'I'm going to have to think about this,' Lenny said. 'I can't put my family in danger.'

'The best way to protect them is to lock up the bad guys, that way you can sleep soundly at night,' Chrissie said.

'I'm damned if I do and damned if I don't,' Lenny said. He sighed and shook his head. 'What choice do I have really?' Lenny asked himself, thinking aloud. 'I hope I don't regret this. Go on Yasmin, let's see the mugshots before I change my mind.'

'Okay. I'll explain what we're going to do,' Yasmin said. 'What I'm using here is called VIPER, or a video identification parade electronic recording. I'm going to show you six images at a time, two rows with three in each. Then each image will be shown individually. If you want to see them again, just ask, or if you need me to go back, just ask.'

'Okay,' Lenny said. He was apprehensive and concerned.

'There's nothing to worry about here,' Chrissie said. 'They are images and nothing more than that.'

'I'm shitting a brick here, and they're only pictures. I would be no good at an old-fashioned line up with the baddies in the building staring back at me.'

'Relax and take your time,' Chrissie said, laughing. 'The old ways of doing line-ups were traumatic for some people. Imagine looking at your rapist through a window. This is a much simpler and less stressful way, and the success rate is almost double.'

'I'll take your word for it,' Lenny said. 'Let's do it.'

'Remember these men may be much older now than they were in the photograph; hair styles, beards, teeth could all be different.'

'Okay, I'll bear that in mind,' Lenny said. 'I'm ready when you are.'

The first six faces appeared. That's when 'reminds me of someone syndrome' kicked in. Part of Lenny's brain wanted to see the men who attacked him, but his self-preservation didn't want to see them again, ever. He looked at each one and shook his head. Yasmin brought the first group up as individuals. None of them were his attackers. He relaxed a little as the second and third groups appeared. None of them were familiar to him. How many images could they have in their records, tens of thousands? What were the odds of him knowing some of them? Another five sets of six mugshots came and were dismissed. The clock ticked by quickly and an hour had gone before he knew it.

'Do you need to stop for a break?' Chrissie asked.

'I'm fine. Let's crack on. I don't recognise anyone so far, although he looks a bit like Mike Tyson,' Lenny said, pointing to the screen.

'He does,' Chrissie agreed, nodding. 'Is it Mike Tyson, Yasmin?'

'I don't put the images of random celebrities into VIPER, amusing as it might be if they were identified for committing a crime,' Yasmin said, shaking her head. She smiled and looked up. 'Imagine if you said it was Mike Tyson who shot you. You could make a fortune.'

'It would be a great story for the lads in the pool team,' Lenny said. 'Guess who shot me the other day. Who? Iron Mike.'

Yasmin smiled and changed the images. Lenny looked and shook his head. They appeared as individuals, and he looked again. *He reminds me of someone.... his brain whispered over and over.*

'Nope,' he said, not listening to the doubts. 'I don't recognise any of them.'

Another six faces appeared. Then another and another. He was beginning to lose the will to live when his eyes were immediately drawn to the top right image. The hair was darker, the eyes younger, fewer lines around the mouth but it was him. Absolutely no doubt about it.

'The top right image, can you bring it up on its own, please?' Lenny said. His mind was screaming at him. *Don't tell them. Don't tell them. Don't tell them. Don't tell them. Don't tell them, it's him.*

'Do you recognise him?' Chrissie asked, standing up. She was alert and interested straight away. 'Take your time.'

'Yes.'

'Tell me how you know him.'

'He contacted me about a Porsche Boxster he was selling. He said his name was Frank McKenna,' Lenny said. 'We arranged a meeting in St Helens and when I arrived, I was attacked. He is that man, there's no doubt about it.'

'For the record,' Chrissie said. 'What did this man do?'

'He is the man who called me and arranged the meeting and he's the man who pulled the trigger. He shot me.'

Yasmin and Chrissie exchanged glances. Yasmin typed into her laptop and several images of the same man appeared. They were all mugshots taken in custody suites over a number of years. Lenny nodded, confirming what he already knew in his own mind.

'That's the shooter, who called himself Frank,' Lenny said, looking at Chrissie. She sighed and nodded but didn't look happy. 'You know him, don't you?'

'Yes,' Chrissie said.

'So, who is he?'

'His name is Lewis Cashman,' Chrissie said. She didn't elaborate but typed a text message into her phone.

'Okay, now you've sent your message, who is he?' Lenny was pissed off that she didn't say any more and it must have shown on his face.

'Let's just say that I was hoping that you wouldn't pick him out.'

'Obviously, I can't change that,' Lenny said. 'He is the man, so tell me who he is.'

'Cashman is bad news. He isn't part of Maddern's outfit.' She shook her head, frustrated. 'He's an enforcer. A freelancer. Maddern must have employed him to attack you. He wasn't there to ask you questions.'

'What do you mean?' Lenny asked, confused. 'They asked me where Maddern's kids were.'

'Maddern could have paid any thug to ask you that and beat you to a pulp, but he didn't. He sent Lewis Cashman.' Chrissie shrugged. 'If Maddern engaged his services, he was sent to gain information and then kill you. With hindsight, I think they must have been disturbed before they had the chance to finish the job.'

'So, they have unfinished business. That's not good news, is it?' Lenny said, shaking his head.

'No. Cashman is not good news.'

'He's a hitman?' Lenny clarified.

'Yes.'

'He's a hitman but he's walking around free?'

'Basically, yes,' Chrissie said, nodding. 'He's linked to several gangland killings, but we've never been able to nail him.'

'How can you know he's a hitman and not bang him up?' Lenny asked, shaking his head.

'Evidence,' Chrissie said. 'It's one thing knowing and another proving it in court. These people are more forensically aware than most coppers in this station and in the unlikely event that there were witnesses, they are intimidated or bribed. It's not as simple as knowing.'

'Okay, okay, so Cashman shot me,' Lenny said, sighing. He felt angry and frustrated. 'My question now is where is he, in or out?'

'He's out,' Chrissie said.

'Fucking brilliant,' Lenny muttered. 'Today is just getting better and better.'

'He lives in Dublin but travels frequently. We suspect he has worked all over the UK.' Chrissie opened a bottle of water as she explained. 'We know he only works with a very select few associates. Yasmin, can you put some images up for me, please.'

'Is he Irish?' Lenny asked, frowning. 'His accent was local. I'm sure it was.'

'He's from Netherley, born and bred in Liverpool,' Chrissie said. 'We think he's been in Dublin for about ten years. He made a lot of enemies over here. There were several local outfits with a grudge against him and there was a price on his head, so he moved to Ireland. It's a lot safer there for him.'

'But he pops back over for work every now and again?' Lenny said, sarcastically. 'You can't arrest him over there, can you?'

'Not without cooperation from the locals, but we can let him know that we know he shot you. That would mean he'd be reluctant to try it again,' Chrissie said. Four new faces appeared on the screen. 'Do you recognise any of them?'

Lenny looked at the screen and nodded. He felt flat and cheated. Lewis Cashman was the man who had shot him, and he was untouchable. His sense of feeling obligated to the police was fading fast.

'Can you put the top two on the left up, please?' Lenny said. Yasmin removed the other four. Lenny looked at them and recalled their faces at the meeting in St Helens. They were bruisers, thick set, broken noses, necks like a bull. 'They are the men who attacked me.'

'You're absolutely sure?'

'Positive. Who are they?'

'The man on the left is Mark Tyrer and the man on the right is Pete Jardine,' Chrissie said, texting another message into her phone. 'Both are associates of Maddern and both are local. Tyrer runs a pool hall in Bootle and Jardine runs a chain of bookies, both of which belong to Barry Maddern. They're under investigation for money laundering and the good news is they're inside.'

'Thank fuck for that,' Lenny sighed. 'That would explain why I'm still walking around?'

'Yes. Cashman won't risk coming over here at the moment. He doesn't know who is talking and what's being said,' Chrissie said. 'Only Maddern, Cashman and those two on the screen would know about you. We'll interview them and they will no doubt deny the attack or make a no comment interview. With your evidence, we can make an attempted murder charge stick. They will be very old men when they get out.'

'What if they have alibis?' Lenny asked. He didn't feel as confident as the detective did. 'I mean cast-iron alibis. What then?'

'There's no such thing as a cast-iron alibi when the victim has identified the attackers, only manufactured alternatives,' Chrissie said. 'Now we know who attacked you, we can track their whereabouts before and after the attack. They will have left holes in any alibi, you can be sure of that. They may have created an alibi for the time of the attack but it's impossible to build one for the days before and after, without leaving mistakes behind. Your statement will trump anything they come up with.'

'And what about Cashman?' Lenny asked.

'If he steps foot across the border, he'll be lifted,' Chrissie said. 'You don't need to worry about him.'

'I wish I had your confidence,' Lenny said. He sighed and drank some water. 'At least the other two are banged up.'

'The conspiracy charges are enough to put them away for ten years, minimum. Attempted murder will double that. They're in jail for a very long time.'

'You need to make sure they stay that way.' Lenny shrugged. 'I feel better knowing they are inside.'

'I'll use every resource available to us to ensure they stay there,' Chrissie said. 'You have my word on that.' Lenny nodded. 'Will you give us a statement?'

'Yes. I must be mad but yes. I will.'

An hour later, Lenny was walking out of the station, feeling mixed emotions. He was elated that Jardine and Tyrer would be interviewed and charged. The odds on them being released in the next twenty years were slim, yet he felt an overwhelming sense of foreboding and he wasn't sure why. When he reached the Jag, he felt a shiver down his spine.

'Someone just walked over your grave, Lenny,' he muttered to himself. He looked around, feeling nervous and vulnerable. Fifty yards away in a black Nissan, two sets of eyes watched his every move.

Chapter 6. The Norris Home.

High up above or down below, when you're too in love to let it go, but if you never try, you'll never know, just what you're worth...

PHIL PARKED THE CAR further down the street than usual because of the number of law enforcement vehicles that were already on the scene. He could see an armed response unit outside the Norris home, which was not a surprise considering Hope had been shot from somewhere close. Phil had owned an air rifle as a teenager, so he knew that as powerful as they are, their range is limited. The search area would be aimed at the surrounding houses. The police were knocking on doors and a few of the neighbours were gathered in small groups being questioned by uniformed officers. A pack of tracksuit-wearing teenagers were hovering on their bikes, smoking and hurling abuse at the police. From behind glass, several neighbours were watching from the safety of their homes. The bedroom windows of overlooking houses were the perfect spot for a sniper to take a shot at someone on the pavement.

Phil was more anxious than he should be, and he wasn't sure why. Heather Norris was a difficult individual and could be abusive and aggressive and her new partner, David Isle, was an arrogant prick. Because the children were already on a Child Protection plan, background checks were needed on David to prove that he presented no threat to their safety. He had three domestic abuse incidents, which ended in NFA, (no further action) and a common assault on his record, which was not enough to stop him moving in with

Heather, but the red flags were waving. He was an unsavoury character at best. There were more red flags in the Norris home than in a communist party conference, but Heather couldn't see it.

Phil knew he was a wrong one and the children felt it too, but Heather was smitten with him. She couldn't see any bad in him; love is blind, they say, and they are invariably right. Phil spent a lot of his working hours trying to convince mothers that their choice of partner was impacting on their children's safety, but it was like talking to a brick wall if they were in love. Heather was an attractive woman, but she had low self-esteem and undervalued her worth. At the first sign of affection from a male, she attached herself to them, without thinking of the long-term ramifications of who they were, and the impact it would have on her children. She went into one shit relationship after another and had a talent for attracting predatory males with violent tendencies. In the middle of the chaos, four children struggled to find enough food in the kitchen. They often went to bed hungry, in the dark, with no lights and no heating and no kiss goodnight. Phil was desperately trying to keep the family together, but Heather wasn't playing ball. If she didn't engage in the protection plan, the next stage would be pre-proceedings for the removal of the children, to place them into care. No one wanted that, but their well-being was paramount. Hungry children in 2023 should not be tolerated.

This was going to be a difficult visit, regardless of what the facts were, just because the parents were difficult at the best of times, and they would no doubt be angry and upset. He took a deep breath and steeled himself; this wasn't about the parents. The safety of the children came first.

Phil climbed out of the vehicle and made his way to the house. There were a couple of journalists hovering near a white van. They were freelancers who listened in to police scanners, waiting for something tragic to happen. Tragedy made good news stories and a twelve-year-old girl being shot in the face was juicy.

'Are you a police officer?' a young woman asked, pointing a microphone towards him. 'What can you tell us about the shooting?'

'I'm not a police officer and I can't tell you anything,' Phil said. He showed his ID to a uniformed officer who was at the garden gate.

'Do you know how the girl is?' she persisted. 'Come on, mate, give us something.'

Phil ignored her and walked up the path. The front door was open, and he could see DI Jane Bennet from the PVPU inside. He ducked beneath the doorframe and stepped into the hallway. Jacob saw him and smiled. He ran to Phil and fist-bumped him.

'Big Phil is in the house!' he shouted.

'Hello Jacob,' Phil said, ruffling his hair. 'How are you doing?'

'Hope got shot in the face, right here,' Jacob said, pointing to his temple. 'There was a bullet stuck in her head. She was bleeding and everything. They took her to the hospital. Do you think she'll die?'

'No Jacob,' Phil said. 'She will be fine. Who went to the hospital with her?' Phil asked.

'My mum,' Jacob said. 'She was crying as well. And she was saying the F-word a lot.'

'I'm sure she was,' Phil said. 'She will be very upset that Hope has been hurt.' Jacob nodded in agreement. 'Where are your sisters?'

'In there talking to a police lady,' Jacob said, gesturing to the living room. 'But they don't want to say anything to her. My friend says, snitches get stitches,' he whispered. 'No one around here talks to the police, he says.'

'Is that what your friend says?' Phil whispered. Jacob nodded. 'If no one ever talks to the police, they will never catch the bad guys. Sounds like a conspiracy of silence for all the wrong reasons, to me,' Phil said, whispering. Jacob looked confused and nodded, smiling.

'It's okay to talk to the police. They're trying to help find out who shot Hope. Let's go in there,' Phil said, stepping into the living room. 'Hello Jane. Don't mind me. Hello girls.'

'Look who is here. Big Phil is in the house!' Jacob shouted again.

'Hiya Phil,' Pru said, waving. She looked nervous. 'Jacob, you're so sad shouting that.'

'Hey Phil,' Paige said.

'You finish your chat with Jane, and we'll catch up when you're done,' Phil said.

He could smell cannabis in the air. It was mingled with cigarettes and stale beer. There were four empty cans of Stella on the floor next to the armchair and flakes of tobacco on a coffee table. The ashtray held four roaches; the stumps of a cannabis joint fashioned from cardboard from a cigarette packet. A bottle of vodka was tucked between the armchair and the settee. Phil picked it up and shook it. There was an inch left in the bottle.

'Where is David?' Phil asked.

'He's smoking cigarettes in the back garden,' Jacob said. Jacob looked agitated. His eyes were flicking between the doorway and the kitchen as if he was waiting for someone to appear.

'Are you okay, little man?' Phil asked, sensing his unease. Jacob shook his head. 'Tell me what's bothering you.'

'Have you got a minute?' Jane interrupted. She approached Phil and lowered her voice. 'They're hiding something and they're not comfortable. I think it might be better if we speak to the children together. They're a bit reluctant to talk to me and they keep asking to speak to you.'

'No problem,' Phil said. He turned to Jacob and gestured to the settee. 'Why don't you sit next to your sisters, and we can all have a chat about what happened. I can see something is bothering you.'

Jacob climbed onto the settee and snuggled up to Paige, who put her arm around him. The love between the siblings was beautiful to see. It went a long way to compensate for their mother's emotional absence.

'Are you sitting comfortably?' Phil asked, joking.

'Yes,' the children said as one.

'Then I'll begin. I want you to tell me what happened this morning from when you woke up until now,' Phil said. 'So, one step at a time. Who woke up first?'

'Hope,' they all said together.

'Who?'

'Hope!' they shouted.

'I think Hope woke up first?' Phil said, shaking his head. 'What do you think?'

'It was Hope!' they shouted. 'We all said it at the same time!' They laughed and nudged each other.

'We're like twins but three of us,' Pru said.

'That's tripods,' Paige said.

'Tripods?' Jacob asked, frowning.

'It's triplets,' Phil said. 'Three of a kind is triplets.'

'We're triplets then,' Paige said. The siblings agreed with a giggle.

'Okay, so you said Hope was awake first?' Phil said.

'Hope is always the first one awake and she wakes us up,' Paige said.

'Then we wake up Jacob,' Pru said. 'Because he's a lazy-bones and wants to stay in bed all the time.'

'I do not!' Jacob protested. 'This morning, I was up before you and Paige.'

'Only because you needed a poo,' Paige said, nodding. 'And it was a stinky poo too,' she added. 'I went to clean my teeth and had to hold my nose.'

'Shut up!' Jacob said, embarrassed. 'You stink all the time, even when you're not in the toilet.'

'Okay, let's not talk about what we do in the bathroom,' Phil said. 'We all need to go to the bathroom at some point in the day.' The children were smirking. 'You said, Hope woke you all up, and then you got dressed?' The children nodded. 'What happened when you came downstairs?'

'Hope made toast and we drank a glass of milk,' Paige said. 'She makes us toast every morning but sometimes there's no bread or milk.'

'Milk makes us grow,' Jacob said, wisely.

'It does. Where was your mum when all this was going on?' Phil asked.

The children looked at each other but didn't speak.

'Have you all lost your tongues?' Phil said, smiling. The children remained quiet. 'Hope will tell me when she comes back from the hospital,' Phil said, playing the game. 'Hope doesn't keep any secrets from me because she knows it's best to tell the truth. Hope always tells me the truth.'

'I tell the truth too. Mum was in bed,' Jacob said. 'She never gets up before school. Hope always gets us ready.'

'Jacob!' Paige said, shaking her head.

'You need to shush,' Pru said, putting her finger to her lips. 'Or we'll be sent to a kids' home. And we'll never be allowed home.'

'Whoah!' Phil said. 'Slow down, you're going too fast,' he said, frowning. 'Who said anything about you being sent to a home?'

The children sat in silence. Jacob picked at his trousers. The girls looked down at their feet.

'Okay. I can see what's going on here,' Phil said. He folded his arms. 'You do know that I'm going to ask Hope, your mum and David if they told you that you would be put in a home if you said anything to me or the police, don't you?'

'No, no, no! Don't ask David,' Jacob said, whispering. 'You can't ask him.'

'Why not?' Phil asked.

'He said that you will take us away and put us in homes and we'll never see each other again.' He leaned forward and summoned Phil closer. 'He said you would put mum in jail if we said bad things about her, like she never gets up in the morning.'

'Did he really?' Phil said, simmering beneath the surface. He could hear David's reedy voice saying those words. The snake. 'Well, he's wrong and he shouldn't be saying things like that to you.'

'What's going on in here?' David Isle asked from the doorway. He glared at the children. 'There's a lot of whispering going on and we don't do whispering in this house.'

'And did you make up that rule?' Phil said.

'It's bad manners to whisper,' David said, shrugging.

'I don't think you've earned the right to lay down the rules just yet,' Phil said, as calmly as he could. 'In fact, you're a long way from that point. We're having a chat with the children, and you're not required, so leave the room and close the door please.'

'You must be joking,' David scoffed. 'Who do you think you are?'

'Phil is the family social worker and if he asks you to leave the room, you leave it. I think you need to go back into the garden and let us do our jobs,' Jane said. She took out her badge and showed it to him. 'Detective Inspector Bennet.' David blushed red and anger flashed in his eyes, but he didn't move. 'Do you have a problem with your hearing?' He looked at her and smiled, shaking his head. 'Then I suggest you leave the room and wait for me in the garden. I want to speak to you when I'm finished here.'

'No problem, detective,' David said. He stared at the children for a second before he turned and left. 'I'll be in the garden.' Phil waited until he was out of earshot.

'You need to listen to me. What David said to you is wrong,' Phil said. 'No one is putting your mum in jail, and no one is taking you away from your home, understand me?'

'But he said you and social services are trying to take us from our mum and if we tell you bad things, we'll go into a home for naughty children,' Paige said. 'My friend at school lives in a home and she hates it. She wants to go home to her mum, but social services won't let her.'

'I'm here to make sure that you stay here with your mum, not take you away,' Phil said. 'You trust me, don't you?' The children nodded. 'You must not listen to anyone telling you anything different. No one is going to put you in a home, okay?'

'Yes.' The girls nodded but Jacob was looking down.

'Jacob?' Phil said. Jacob looked unsure. 'You need to know that what I'm saying are the facts. What David said is a lie.' Jacob shrugged. 'What are you thinking?'

'David is mean and when you're gone, he's going to be mad because we told you stuff,' Jacob said, his voice quiet and quivering. 'He will be mean again.'

'When was he mean?' Phil asked.

'Today and all the time, especially when mum isn't here.' Jacob shifted uncomfortably. 'He says mean things when mum isn't here.'

'You said that he was mean today?' Phil said. 'What did he do that is mean?'

'He said we were like a plague of locusts and called us brats,' Pru said.

'And he said he was going to give Hope a fucking good hiding,' Jacob whispered.

'Jacob!' Paige said, shaking her head. 'You shouldn't say that word.'

'That's what he said, not me,' Jacob said.

'It's okay,' Phil said. 'You're just telling me what he said. I asked you a question and you told me the truth. Don't worry about it.' Jacob nodded and looked relieved. 'When did he say that?'

'This morning,' Paige said. 'We drank all the milk, and he was mad but there wasn't much milk anyway.'

'Okay, so he was mad about the milk, but why did he say that to Hope?' Phil asked.

'He called us brats and Hope said she was going to tell our dad and he would batter him,' Pru said. 'Our dad would batter him, too.'

'This was before you left for school?' Phil asked. The children nodded. 'Before Hope was shot?'

'Yes,' Jacob said. 'He's mean. When mum went with Hope in the ambulance, David said we mustn't say anything bad about mum or him or we would be taken to a home and never see each other again.'

'Well, David is badly mistaken,' Phil said. He ruffled Jacob's hair. 'No one is going to a home, okay?' The children nodded. 'I want you to forget you ever heard that because it's not true.'

'Why is he saying that?' Jacob asked.

'David probably told you that so you wouldn't tell me that he swore at Hope but what he's saying is a lie. Lies mask the truth and we need to know the truth, don't we?' The children nodded.

'He told the policeman a lie too,' Jacob said, whispering again.

'What did he say?' Jane asked. Jacob looked at Phil.

'You can tell Jane what he said,' Phil said. 'She's a boss at the police station. All the other police officers have to do what she says.'

'Really?' Jacob said, glancing at Jane. She nodded and smiled. Jacob was clearly impressed. 'Are you the boss of everyone?'

'Not everyone,' Jane said. 'But I'm in charge here, so you can whisper to me. What did he say that was a lie?'

'The policeman asked if there was an airgun in the house,' Jacob said. 'And he said no. That was a lie.'

Chapter 7. Storage King

M*ama never loved her much, that's why she shies away from human affection...*

THE DUTY MANAGER AT Storage King, Warrington, was sitting in his office, sorting through a stack of applications. Rupert Stokes had been employed there for five years, and he was coasting along, unmotivated and uninspired. Hiring staff was a relentless task and it was boring him to sleep; it was the worst part of the job. Turnover was high and finding good employees was almost impossible. When he read a decent application, he then searched for the candidate on social media. It was quicker than conducting an interview and their pictures talked a million words. There was no bullshit to wade through. It was all there in digital detail for the world to see.

Social media profiles told him volumes. Here I am, a fucked-up individual who craves attention on Facebook and has serious bouts of anxiety and depression and can't hold down a job. Or I'm a huge pisspot who thinks it's funny to call in sick and then post pictures of themselves partying until there are no parties left. And then there were the racists, sexist, misogynistic idiots, who vented their spleen online and wondered why they never got an interview. It wasn't hard to understand why some people never heard back from prospective employers. Some of the Instagram generation didn't have the brains they were born with.

The exodus of European labour caused by Brexit had caused a vacuum and the current workforce were picky and fickle. Sitting behind a desk on minimum wage was not an attractive career option for most but some people would take the job just to earn a few quid, while they looked for a better position. The job entailed some customer interaction and a level of online knowledge, but it wasn't like working for NASA. There was no rocket science involved. Match the customer to the right lock and leave them to it. He needed to hire someone for the nightshifts, preferably over fifty and retired from their career. They were less likely to be on a bender at the weekends or phone in sick at the last minute. He was tired of having to cover shifts himself because the lazy bastards couldn't be bothered coming to work. A knock on the door disturbed him. The door opened and Vanessa peered around the frame, looking worried.

'You had better come out here, Rupert,' she said.

'Can't you see, I'm busy?' he sighed. 'Why do I need to come out there?'

'There are uniformed policemen and detectives here,' she said. 'Lots of them and they want to talk to you.'

'What the fuck?' Rupert said, standing up. 'I'm rushed off my feet here. What do they want?'

'You look busy, Rupert!' she said, shaking her head. Vanessa pointed to the security monitors. 'Have you not noticed them on the car park? You're supposed to monitor the cameras. Look how many of them are here.'

'Are you exaggerating again?' Rupert looked up and saw several marked police vehicles, two minibuses full of uniformed officers and a forensic van. 'Are they at the right address? What the fuck is going on?'

'I don't know but they're not messing around, and the guy in charge is at the desk and he has got a shitty attitude,' Vanessa said. 'You'd better come and talk to them.'

Rupert straightened his tie and walked into the reception area. Police officers were crawling all over the building, some climbing the stairs and others waiting to use the lift.

'Excuse me, don't go up there, please!' Rupert said, shocked. 'Where are they going?'

'They're going wherever I tell them to.' The detective in charge was standing next to the reception desk, talking to some other plain-clothed officers. He held up his warrant card and handed Rupert a warrant. 'I'm DCI French. This is a warrant to search unit fifty-six on the first floor. Do you have a key to the lock?'

'No,' Rupert said. 'We don't have access to any of the rented space. They're secured by the clients, and we only enter them if the rent isn't paid, or the key is lost. What are you looking for?'

'I'm afraid we can't disclose any information until we've searched the unit.'

'I'll need to call head office to get permission,' Rupert protested. 'I can't let you just break into a client's unit.'

'I'm not asking for your permission. That is your permission,' DCI French said, pointing to the warrant. 'I need you and your staff to stay in the office. We're going to need to go through your records when we're done searching.'

'Shouldn't I be there when you're searching?' Rupert muttered. The DCI was already heading for the stairs, and he didn't reply. 'Okay, help yourself. Do what you like. Fucking cheek!' he said to himself. 'Who does he think he is?'

'A detective chief inspector,' Vanessa said, nodding. She craned her neck to watch him walking upstairs. 'Very rugged. He could handcuff me any night of the week.'

'You give away far too much information,' Rupert said, frowning. 'That's an image in my head now and it won't ever go away.'

'Pervert,' Vanessa said.

Rupert and Vanessa were left in the reception, feeling a little shellshocked.

'Can they just come in and search a unit?' Vanessa asked.

'Don't ask me. I'm just the manager,' Rupert moaned. 'I wasn't given much choice, was I?'

'He was very assertive,' Vanessa said, nodding. 'He's quite sexy in a bossy kind of way. And you didn't put up much of a fight, to be honest. A bit wimpy, to be honest.'

'Shut up, Vanessa,' Rupert said, storming back into his office. 'The last thing I need is you on my case. Keep your eye on reception. I'm going to call head office.'

'What are they doing up there?' Vanessa asked. 'Why do they need all those police officers?'

'That is a search warrant, so I'm assuming they're searching for something, so can you save any more stupid questions for another day please?' Rupert said, slamming the door.

'Narky knickers,' Vanessa said, picking up her phone. She went to the front window and took three selfies with the police vehicles on the car park in the background and shared them to her Instagram. 'Wait until my besties see this. They will be so well-jell.'

She shared the images on Facebook and Instagram and was watching the likes and notifications coming in. Two detectives walked down the stairs and approached her. One was male and the other female, both thirty-something, dressed in jeans and tee-shirts with stab-vests over the top.

'You guys must be expecting trouble,' Vanessa joked but they didn't laugh. 'We don't get many stabbings in here.'

'Do you have access to customer information?' the female asked.

'I have limited access to personal information, but the manager does. Rupert is in his office,' Vanessa said, walking behind the desk. 'Did you find something?'

'We're not at liberty to say,' the male said, gesturing to the door marked manager. 'Is he in there?'

'I'll see if he can see you,' Vanessa said, trying to sound important, but the detectives had opened the door and were already in the office. They closed the door as she approached.

'Fucking charming,' she muttered. 'The first exciting thing to ever happen in this shithole, and everyone wants to keep it a secret!' She went back to her social media for comfort.

In the office, Rupert was talking to his area manager, who was having a fit about bad publicity for the company. Rupert wished he had never made the phone call. His boss was so anal, everything was about him. He was surprised that the detectives had barged into his office without knocking. The detectives gestured to Rupert to end his phone call. He did so, reluctantly.

'I was on the phone to my boss and he's not happy about this,' Rupert said, sitting up straight.

'I'm DC Evans, this is DC Talbot,' the male detective said, ignoring what he had said. 'We need all the information you have on unit fifty-six.'

'This is most irregular,' Rupert said, shaking his head. 'Are you sure your warrant gives you access to our customer database?'

'Following our search, we are now conducting a murder enquiry,' Evans said. Rupert felt like he had been slapped. 'I would expect any decent business to cooperate fully with such an enquiry. We could have all your computers seized and removed if you have an issue with sharing information?'

'No,' Rupert said. 'There's no need to be rash.' He blushed. 'I don't have any issues with it. I'm only too happy to help but I am mindful of the data protection breach, that's all. I'm sure your warrant covers it from our perspective.'

'Good,' Talbot said, approaching his desk and pulling up a chair next to him. She looked at him, his expression blank. 'Unit fifty-six?'

'Yes, yes, yes. Unit fifty-six.' Rupert typed in the unit number. The information appeared on the screen.

'It was hired and paid for by a company called Merseyside Security Systems,' Rupert said. 'They paid for twenty-four months in advance.'

'That's one of Maddern's companies,' Evans said. Talbot nodded. 'They paid for two years in advance?' Rupert nodded and reddened. 'Is that normal?'

'It happens,' Rupert said, shrugging.

'How did they pay?' Talbot asked.

'On a pre-loaded Mastercard,' Rupert said, staring at the screen.

'Not linked to any bank account?'

'No. I'm afraid not,' Rupert said, feeling a little smug.

'So, you have no idea where the money came from?' Talbot asked, frowning. 'I thought you had to do stringent checks on where funds come from?'

'It's a perfectly legitimate method of payment,' Rupert said.

'It's called money laundering,' Evans said, watching Rupert's response. The colour drained from his face.

'Why would a security company be laundering money?' Rupert asked, shocked.

'Because they're a front for an organised criminal gang,' Evans said. 'Drug dealers.'

'You're joking,' Rupert said, pretending to be more shocked than he was.

'This is no joke,' Talbot said. 'A quick Google search would have flagged up the company as disreputable.'

'Look,' Rupert stammered. 'I'm not here to investigate companies and decide if their money is clean or not. I take bookings and payment and make sure no one breaks into the customer's unit. That's it.'

'There is a chest freezer in that unit,' Talbot said. 'What did you think was in it?'

'I didn't know what was in there,' Rupert said. 'It's none of my business.'

'It becomes your business if there's a body in it,' Evans said. 'The victim didn't fall into the freezer, which means they were murdered by the people who paid for the unit two years in advance on a pre-paid card, without any questions being asked.'

'Do you see where this is going?' Talbot asked.

'I haven't done anything wrong,' Rupert protested. 'Why are you making me feel like this is my fault?'

'Because you're in charge of the facility. When was the last time anyone entered that unit?' Talbot asked.

'No one has,' Rupert said, showing them the access log.

'What?' Talbot said, shaking her head. 'Never?'

'Never. Not since they hired the unit.'

'Bollocks,' Evans said.

'I beg your pardon?' Rupert said, shocked.

'There's a clean oblong-shaped patch on the floor about the size of a trunk, which tells me something was taken from that unit recently?'

'Not according to the log,' Rupert said, pointing to the screen. 'Every visit is logged in here. This says no one has been into unit fifty-six.'

'Okay,' Talbot said. 'We're going to need all your CCTV footage going back as far as you can.'

'It wipes clean daily,' Rupert said, shrugging.

'Daily?' Evans snapped.

'Yes.' Rupert sighed. 'This is a storage facility. It's a big building filled with stuff. There are no people in it. We don't keep recordings of empty corridors for more than a day. What's the point?'

'It may be a building full of stuff but there is a dead person in it, and they were murdered,' Talbot said.

'Is there really a dead person up there?' Rupert muttered. 'In the unit?'

'Yes. In a freezer.'

'Fucking hell,' Rupert sighed. 'My boss will flip his lid. He's a twat at the best of times, this will blow his head off.'

'Listen to me, Roger,' Evans said.

'Rupert.'

'What?'

'My name is Rupert.'

'Okay Rupert. Someone moved something large from that unit recently, probably a trunk or chest of some kind. Now, I'm guessing that person is the same one who tipped us off about unit fifty-six.'

'You had a tip off?'

'Yes. We didn't come to just any storage facility and pick the unit at random,' Talbot said, shaking her head. 'You need to keep up.'

'I don't know what you're saying,' Rupert said. 'This is a shock.'

'Let me spell it out, so that you can understand exactly what is going on,' Evans said. 'Someone has been in that unit recently. Their visit has not been logged, so one of your staff let them in without logging the visit. Why would they do that?'

'I don't know?' Rupert said.

'They failed to log a visit to a unit with a dead body in it. Does that seem like a coincidence to you?'

'I don't know anything about these things.'

'I think we're going to need to investigate you and your staff, because someone is cooperating with a serious organised crime gang. They let someone in without recording it,' Talbot said. 'We need to speak to all your staff. Bank accounts never lie.'

'What?' Rupert muttered.

'Get your boss on the telephone and tell him to get here and you need to call in all your staff,' Talbot said. 'We need to speak to them all. If anyone can't get here or has a problem with it, we can arrange for them to be interviewed at a police station of their choice.'

Chapter 8. Sam

SAM NEEDED MILK AND a bottle of wine. The baseline from the cuckooed flat beneath him had gone quiet, which was a relief but also begged the question of what the fuck they were up to down there. He looked out of the window, hoping there was a police car there, but the road was quiet. There were three bicycles and an electric scooter on the path leading to the building. Their riders were nowhere to be seen but he could guess where they were. He contemplated waiting for a while before leaving his flat and getting into his car but decided that he wasn't going to allow a bunch of teenage thugs to dictate when he could come and go from his home. Fuck em, he thought.

Sam opened the door and walked to the top of the stairs. He could hear voices at the bottom of the stairwell. They were young and local. An older voice was speaking over them, aggressive and menacing. They all began laughing, their voices echoing up the stairwell. He thought about going back inside but overruled it. If anyone said anything out of order, he would call the police. He was certain someone in the building had already alerted them to the invasion, but if the property was empty, the police usually deemed it as the landlord's problem. They were effectively squatters with squatters' rights and it could take weeks to evict them. Having said that, if they were causing a nuisance, threatening people or conducting illegal activities, the police would attend eventually but there was no guarantee of shifting them from the property.

Sam walked down the stairs, focused on the front door. He glanced in the direction of Les's flat and saw four tracksuit-clad teens in the hallway, talking to an older man in his thirties. Sam recognised one of the teenagers. He guessed the older guy was in charge of proceedings. They were looking at several pairs of new Nike trainers, handing them around like they were fragile. The man stopped talking and eyed Sam suspiciously as if he was the one who shouldn't be there. The teenagers followed his gaze and looked at Sam. They all glared at him.

'Everything okay?' the man asked, sarcastically. 'You never seen a pair of trainers before?'

'I'm ticketty-boo, thank you. Nice kicks,' Sam said. He looked away and walked to the door. The voices turned to whispers. He opened the door and stepped outside into the cold drizzle. The daylight was fading fast. He reached his car, and the teenagers came out of the flats and picked up their bikes; the lad on the e-scooter whizzed by at full speed, obviously in a rush. They all looked nervous. One of the boys caught his eye and nodded. It was Andrew Head, son of Tony and Sandra. Sam nodded back and felt guilt creeping through his soul.

Your dad is never coming home, he thought; I lured him to his death and I'm not sorry. Guilty, yes. Sorry, no.

The boys said goodbye to each other and rode in different directions. Andrew Head rode along the pavement towards Sam. He was wearing brand new white Nikes. Sam pointed at them.

'Nice trainers,' Sam said.

'Thanks,' Andrew said, blushing.

'Must have cost a bob or two?'

'They're well expensive, mate,' Andrew said, proudly.

'You haven't taken them from the bloke in Les's flat, have you?' Sam asked, concerned. 'He's bad news.'

'He's alright,' Andrew said.

'What have you got to do for those trainers, Andrew?'

'Mind your own fucking business. Sorry. I can't stop to talk. I've got to be somewhere.' he cycled off as fast as he could pedal.

'I bet you have somewhere to be,' Sam muttered getting into his car. He closed the door and glanced at his building. The older man was standing in the doorway, staring. He didn't say a word, but his expression said, mind your own business. Sam looked away and drove off. It was none of his business. If the local dealers had recruited another batch of naive teenagers, what could he do about it? The police couldn't stop them, so he had fuck all chance of doing anything.

Sam switched on the radio and listened to the news. There was the usual spattering of doom and gloom. Wildfires across Europe, Putin still blowing up women and children in Ukraine, Israel and Hamas bombing the shit out of civilians, and the economy more fucked than it was last month and then the local news came on. A different presenter began to inform Liverpool and the Northwest that they were more fucked than the people down south just because that was the way it was. Levelling up was a load of old tripe but who believed it anyway? Then a headline hit him like a brick in the face.

'A dismembered body found in a storage facility in Warrington is thought to be connected to the arrests of an OCG from Liverpool and has all the marks of a gangland killing. The police are appealing for anyone with information to come forward or ring Crimestoppers...'

They never found his body, Sam thought. Tony had been missing with no activity on his phone or bank account, so he was dead, obviously but they never found a body, why?

Because it was hidden in a storage facility in Warrington. Tony was going to be coming home after all.

Chapter 9. The Hospital

HEATHER NORRIS BOUGHT a bottle of water from a vending machine and went back to the relatives' room, where she was waiting for Hope to come out of theatre. The pellet in her temple was embedded in the soft tissue and removing it with tweezers would damage the delicate tissue and scar her. The doctors were acutely mindful that she was a young girl and scarring her face was not an option. A surgeon was consulted, and he said he could remove the projectile without scarring if they did it immediately. Heather was in no fit state to argue or ask questions, so she signed the forms and Hope was prepped and taken to surgery.

Heather looked at her reflection in the window. She had thrown on a pink jogging suit and tied her dark hair into a ponytail. She was still a size twelve, even after giving birth to four children, but David called her podgy. Her forehead was showing signs that her Botox was wearing off. She would need to put a few hundred quid aside to get it topped up again. And her lips needed doing too. It hurt like fuck last time despite the dental-block injections and she bled for ages. She pouted at her reflection. Not bad considering she'd had two minutes to get ready before the ambulance turned up. She checked her fake Rolex. Hope had been gone nearly an hour. She had been gone longer than she expected but the nurses couldn't tell her anymore. The door opened and the doctor stepped in. He smiled.

'Hope is out of surgery,' he said. He was a big man in blue scrubs. 'She's a little groggy but the pellet was removed, and the surgeon says the scar will be almost invisible in twelve months. The police have taken the pellet away as evidence.'

'Oh, thank heavens above. Can I see her?' Heather asked.

'Of course,' the doctor said. 'Come on. I'll take you to her. She might be a little dopey for a while as the anaesthetic wears off.'

'As long as she is okay,' Heather said. 'That's all that matters. I've been going out of my mind in here. It's like torture waiting.'

'Heather, we need a word,' Phil Molt said, from the doorway. His long raincoat made him look even taller than he was. It was wet and dripping onto the floor. DI Jane Bennet was behind him, and two female uniformed officers were in the corridor.

'Fuck off, Phil, not right now,' Heather snapped. 'My daughter has just had surgery and I'm going to see her. I'm sick of you hanging around my life like a bad smell. Leave me alone. Whatever shite you want to talk about can wait until I've seen Hope.'

'I'm afraid it won't wait, Heather.' Jane said. 'I'm detective inspector Bennet from the PVPU. Your daughter was shot. It's a very serious matter and we need to ask you some questions.'

'Oh, for fuck's sake. Are you for real? I want to see my daughter!' Heather shouted. Her voice echoed down the corridor and startled nurses peered at the group. 'You two can fuck off! Leave me alone!'

'Is this really necessary?' the doctor asked, trying to calm the situation. 'I think a little compassion wouldn't go amiss. Her daughter has just had surgery.'

'I'll show all the compassion in the world once I have arrested whoever shot Hope, and we're here to determine who that was, so absolutely yes, it is necessary,' Jane said.

A nurse approached from the corridor. She tapped the doctor on the shoulder, and they talked in whispers as they walked away.

'I've got nothing to say to either of you. I want to see my daughter.' Heather folded her arms and tried to barge past Phil. The uniformed officers held her. 'Get off me, you fucking dyke!'

'There's no need for that, Heather. Answer a couple of questions and you can see Hope,' Phil said. 'But you need to calm down and behave yourself. They won't tolerate aggression and abuse in here. If you don't want to be thrown out, calm down.'

'Oh, my god. You're doing my fucking head in. What do you want, Phil?' Heather asked, trying to restrain herself. 'I'm worried about my little girl and you're here asking your fucking questions. Questions, questions, questions. When do you ever have anything good to say, Phil?'

'This is not the time to have a go at me, Heather. I'm just doing my job,' Phil said. 'Hope was shot in the face. We have to ask questions, surely you can see that?'

'Tell this bitch to let go of me and I'll answer your questions.' Jane nodded at the officers, and they released their grip. 'What do you want to know?' Heather sighed, tiring of struggling.

'Did you know David Isle owns an air rifle?' Phil asked. 'Don't lie to us, Heather. You will make things far worse if you do.'

'What?' Heather mumbled. She shook her head. 'You don't think...'

'We don't think anything yet,' Phil said. 'Answer the question. Did you know he owns an air rifle?'

'Yes, of course,' Heather said, nodding. She pushed a stray hair back behind her ears. 'He keeps it in the wardrobe.'

'In your bedroom?' Phil asked.

'Yes. So, the kids can't mess with it.'

'Did he take it out of the wardrobe this morning?' Jane asked. Heather shook her head and made to speak but no words came out. 'The only place in your house where a rifle could be fired at the pavement is from your bedroom window.' Heather looked terrified. Her bottom lip quivered. 'You were in bed, weren't you?'

'Yes.'

'Then if David fired at Hope, you were there,' Jane said. Heather didn't reply. 'Am I to assume that you watched him take out the rifle, open the window and shoot at your daughter?'

'Are you off your head? How can you think that?' Heather whispered. 'What type of mother do you think I am?'

'Answer the question, Heather,' Phil said. 'Did David take his gun out of the wardrobe this morning?'

'No,' she said, shaking her head. Phil could see doubt in her eyes. She was frightened. 'Why would he shoot at Hope, for fuck's sake?'

'They had an argument in the kitchen at breakfast and David threatened Hope with a 'fucking good hiding'.' Phil waited for a reply, but none came. 'He called them selfish brats and Hope gave him some cheek.' Phil waited to let the information sink in. 'Did he go near that wardrobe this morning?'

'No.'

'Are you absolutely sure?' Phil asked.

'Absolutely,' Heather said.

'Heather Norris, I'm arresting you for grievous bodily harm,' Jane said, taking out cuffs. 'You do not have to say anything...'

Heather didn't hear the rest of the caution. Her head was spinning. 'Phil, what are they doing?' Heather asked as she was cuffed. 'Why is she doing this to me?'

'I told you not to lie, Heather,' Phil said. 'David has admitted to having a rifle, but he claims he didn't touch it. One of the neighbours says he saw him looking out of the window.'

'I saw him at the window. He was looking at a local lad who sells drugs to school kids on their way into school. He was across the road,' Heather protested. 'David hates dealers.'

'Why didn't you mention that?' Jane asked.

'He told me not to say anything. That he would get the blame.' She broke down in tears. 'He said Hope must have been shot by one of the neighbours. I didn't know he had threatened her. Honestly, I didn't know!'

'You were in the room in bed,' Jane said. 'If he shot at Hope, you saw it happen. If you're sticking to your story and covering for him, that makes you complicit in the assault.'

'He didn't take the gun out of the wardrobe,' Heather said. 'I wouldn't lie there and let him shoot out of the window, would I?'

'Save it for the police station,' Phil said. He sensed Heather was lying for whatever reason she had. A misplaced sense of loyalty or was she covering her own back because she watched it happen? Whatever her reasons were, she was in trouble. 'You should not have let him bring a gun into your home. Don't think about David now. You need to think about your children, Heather, because this is a massive fuck up. Absolutely massive.'

'Oh, come on, Phil. I wouldn't hurt Hope,' Heather shouted as she was held by uniformed officers. 'I might not be the perfect mum, but I wouldn't see my kids being hurt. Phil, you know me. You know I wouldn't hurt my children!' Phil looked away. 'Phil, Phil, don't do this to me!'

The doctor and a surgeon approached in a hurry. 'What is happening to Miss Norris?'

'She's being spoken to down at the station,' Jane said. 'What's the problem?'

'Hope is being taken back to surgery. She's not responding as she should. We need to investigate immediately.'

'Meaning what, exactly?' Phil asked.

'What's wrong with her?' Heather shouted at the top of her voice. 'Get these fucking cuffs off me. Let me see my daughter!'

'We think she has a bleed on the brain,' the surgeon said. 'I need to operate right now.'

'If you need permission, you have it, don't they, Heather?' Phil said.

'Yes. Of course.' Heather nodded; tears steaked her face. 'Do what you have to do. I want to see her!'

'You can't see her,' the doctor said. 'There isn't time. Wait in the relatives' room and we'll come to see you as soon as we have any news. I am not happy about her being in cuffs while she's waiting.'

'Take the cuffs off her and take her in there, please,' Jane asked the uniformed officers. 'Make sure she doesn't move from there.'

'No, no, no, don't you stop me from seeing my daughter!' The officers frogmarched her down the corridor to the waiting room. 'Get these bitches off me! Phil, you fucking bastard!'

They went through the double doors into reception area and her voice became muffled. 'Phil, Phil, Phil, you bastard!'

'What a nightmare,' Phil muttered.

'You can't do anything about any of this,' Jane said. 'Don't listen to her.'

'I'm not worried about what Heather Norris thinks of me, but I told her children that I would make sure they stay with their mother,' Phil said. 'If she watched David Isle shoot her daughter, she's not going to be going home tonight, is she?'

'If that's the case, it's very unlikely that she'll be going home for a while,' Jane said. 'I need to go and interview him at the station. Will you keep me informed, please?'

'Of course,' Phil said, nodding. 'I'm going to wait and see what happens to Hope. Fingers crossed she comes through this.'

'You know what this means if she doesn't, don't you?' Jane asked. Phil nodded. There was no need to reply. It would be murder.

Chapter 10. Lenny

Here in my car, I know I've started to think, about leaving tonight, although nothing seems right...

LENNY DROVE FROM SPEKE to Tuebrook in good time. He wanted to catch the first lots at the car auction. There weren't many physical auctions left now; most of them had moved online. Tuebrook was a good auction for Liverpool dealers as it was central, so moving vehicles around was cheaper than buying from Manchester or London. It was a four-acre site packed full of quality used vehicles, just a stone's throw from the city centre. He parked up and climbed out of the Jaguar, locking it as he walked away. It was busy and he could feel the buzz already.

'Good to see you, Lenny,' a traffic director said, waving. He was wearing a fur trapper's hat with ear flaps and an orange high-viz jacket.

'And you, Sid.' Lenny waved back and walked towards the auction rooms. 'It's a cold one.'

'My feet are like blocks of ice.' Sid stamped his feet to reinforce the point. 'I'll get a brew and warm up once the sale starts.'

'Make sure you do,' Lenny said.

'Hey Lenny Ray,' a voice shouted from his left. He turned to see Wally Jackson a few cars away, drinking a cup of something hot. Steam was rising from his cup. He was wearing his dark sheepskin jacket and had four sovereign rings on his fingers that made him look like a dodgy dealer. 'How the devil, are you?'

'Alright, Wally,' Lenny shouted. 'Good day for it.'

'What are you doing here, I heard you got shot?' Wally shouted. Heads turned and looked towards him. People pointed and talked about him. He flushed red and walked quickly towards Wally. Wally smiled. He had two gold teeth, and his too-black hair was swept back and gelled. 'I heard you were nearly dead, mate.' Curious onlookers watched with interest.

'It was touch and go for a while,' Lenny said, nodding.

'Horrible bastards. Cowards they are. Barry Maddern got his comeuppance inside though.' Wally chuckled at the thought. 'That was fucking great news. I had a few pints when I heard that he had been finished. Anyway, back from the dead, Lenny. How are you doing?'

'Keep it down, for fuck's sake,' Lenny said, shushing him. 'I don't want everyone to know what happened. People might start feeling sorry for me and giving a shit.' Lenny joked.

'At a car auction?' Wally said, frowning. 'No one has any sympathy here. They're all greedy bastards with no conscience.'

'We wouldn't have it any other way, Wally,' Lenny said.

'Are you buying or selling?'

'Buying,' Lenny said. 'I'm not desperate for stock but I wanted to get back in the saddle.'

'I'll give you a good price for that F-Type you're driving,' Wally said, gesturing towards the car. 'Nice motor, mate.'

'You wouldn't know a good price if it came up and bit you on the arse,' Lenny said. 'She's not for sale.'

'Can't say I blame you.' Wally sipped his drink. 'It's good to see you, mate. We were worried about you for a while.'

'Behave yourself. Don't go getting all sentimental on me,' Lenny said. 'You'll ruin your reputation as a proper twat.' He patted Wally on the back. 'Good to see you too. I'm going to get a coffee before they kick off.'

'See you later,' Wally said. 'I want the grey Range Rover. Don't bid on it.'

'If you like it, I wouldn't touch it with a barge pole. It probably won't get me home,' Lenny called after him as he approached the burger van. The smell of fried onions reached him. A young black woman with braids looked up and her smile widened. 'Hello Della. Have you missed me?'

'Lenny!' She ran out of the van and hugged him, kissing him on the cheek. She smelled of Chanel and bacon. A strange mix. 'It's so good to see you!' she said. 'We heard you were shot?' More people looked over at him and stared. It appeared being shot gave him celebrity status of sorts 'Are you okay now?'

'They tried to patch me up, but I've got a hole in my belly now, so if I drink coffee, you will have to follow me around with a mop.'

'Shut up!' Della laughed. 'Are you hungry?'

'Starving.'

'What are you having to eat?'

'I've been warned not to risk the food here, but I'll try a coffee,' Lenny said.

'Fuck off, Lenny or I'll shoot you too,' Della said, climbing back into the van. 'Seriously though, I'm glad mad Maddern got wasted. He was a first-class wanker in my book.' She smiled. 'Do you want a cheeseburger or not?'

'I'll take the gamble. This once,' Lenny said. Della frowned and shook her head. 'Extra ketchup and mustard.'

'On the way,' Della said, placing a meat patty onto a bun. 'Are you buying or selling?'

'Buying today.'

'Good luck.' She handed him a burger in a napkin and a coffee. Lenny tapped his card on the reader. 'Good to see you back, Lenny. How's your Jo?'

'She's good thank you. Still saving the planet, one child at a time.'

'She's an angel. Tell her I was asking after her.'

'I will. Thanks, Della,' Lenny said, taking a bite from his burger. 'Is there any beef in this beefburger?'

'Fuck off, Lenny!'

Lenny walked away laughing and made his way to the stands in the salesroom. Slate grey clouds rolled across the sky, looking moody and ominous. Fuel floated on top of a puddle, iridescent hues of blues and greens of a mallard's throat. He pushed the door and stepped inside. It was warm and smelled of petrol and exhaust fumes. The seats were tiered twelve benches high, and he picked a spot at the top of the stairs on an empty bench. He wanted to chill and not get involved in dealer chitchat. The elevated position gave him the best view of everything coming through the sale and who was bidding. It was important to work out who was desperate for stock and had money to spend or you could end up paying too much for a vehicle. Some dealers would bid just to push the price up. He climbed the steps and nodded hello to a few familiar faces. Several people said it was good to see him back in business and he felt good to be back.

He sat down and put his coffee on the bench next to him and finished his burger. Opening the auction app, he browsed the vehicles that would be coming through the saleroom. There were a couple of possibles if the prices were right, but he wasn't blown away by anything. It felt good to be back on the benches watching the auction and soaking up the atmosphere. It was always an entertaining afternoon surrounded by characters with colourful language and cutting banter. If two of the bigger dealers went head-to-head over a vehicle, the air could turn blue. There was no love lost once the bidding began.

Lenny sipped his coffee and took in the atmosphere. The auctioneer took his position at a lectern beside the office window and the first vehicle appeared from his right. It was an Evoque on a 15-plate but the mileage was way too high. His attention was drawn by a big man in a black beanie hat, climbing the steps. He was conspicuous because of his size and the fact he was wearing mirrored Ray-Bans. It was dull and raining outside and even the most ardent posers wouldn't wear shades in the salesroom. A few of the dealers followed him with their eyes. This man was trying to hide his appearance but was actually attracting attention to himself instead. Lenny felt a shiver run down his spine. His instincts told him something was about to happen. Something bad.

The man reached the top of the steps and walked along the empty bench until he was next to Lenny on his left. He sat down without saying a word. Lenny could smell Creed aftershave. Three-hundred pounds a bottle scent. Lenny eyed him and sipped his coffee. The man was wearing a Hugo Boss jacket and jeans and mustard coloured Rockport trainers, standard gangster gear in the city. The man was a caricature of a nineties dealer. Lenny thought he probably had a few shiny shell-suits in his wardrobe; he almost laughed at the thought, but the situation wasn't funny.

A second man dressed in a black leather overcoat walked up the opposite steps and walked along the empty bench until he was next to Lenny on his right. Clearly a planned pincer movement and a little too obvious for an onlooker. He sat down and stared at Lenny. If they were trying to intimidate, they were succeeding but Lenny didn't show it. Lenny met his gaze and sipped his coffee.

'Have you got a problem?' Lenny asked him. He glared back at Lenny.

'Hello Lenny.' Sunglasses said. 'We have got a problem as it happens. You're our problem, Lenny.'

'You know who I am. Do I know you?' Lenny replied, nonchalantly. He was calm on the exterior but inside was fixing to run as fast as he could across the benches.

'No, you don't know us, but you know friends of ours and they're pissed off with you. You must be a very stupid man,' the man with the sunglasses said, without turning his head. The second man continued to stare at Lenny. Lenny figured he wasn't a full shilling, but it felt like his eyes were burning into his head. 'We've been watching you and we saw you go to the Matrix unit at Speke. So, why would you go into a police station of your own accord?' Lenny didn't reply. 'We figured that you must have gone there telling tales about people. What have you been saying to the police?'

'I said quite a lot, if I'm honest but it's got fuck all to do with you.' Lenny sipped his coffee.

'That makes you a grass. No one likes a grass around here,' the second man said. His voice sounded like he had gravel in his throat. 'Snitches get stitches.'

'Snitches get stitches. Is that the best you can come up with?' Lenny laughed, which confused the men. They looked at each other, not sure how to react. 'That's a classic. I think I first heard it on the playground at primary school when one of my friends told a teacher something about another kid,' Lenny said. He sipped his coffee and tried to remain calm. On the inside, he was flapping. The bullet wound ached. He was just metres away from dozens of people, yet he felt isolated and vulnerable. He saw Wally Jackson looking up at him from the lower benches. He frowned as if to ask if he was alright. Lenny shook his head almost imperceptibly to say that he wasn't alright.

'You heard that in primary school?' Sunglasses said, nodding. 'You should have fucking listened then, shouldn't you?'

'You clearly weren't listening at the time,' the second man said. 'Or you wouldn't be a fucking grass today.'

'What is this?' Lenny asked, smiling. 'Are you like a gruesome-twosome double act sent to scare people?' Sunglasses turned his head to face Lenny for the first time since sitting down. 'Don't tell me someone has paid you to come here and try to shut me up, because you're way too late for that party.'

'Are we, really?' Sunglasses said, nodding. His face was like thunder; Lenny could tell that he wasn't enjoying the experience. Things weren't going as they had planned it.

'Yes, really.' Lenny checked his watch. 'I reckon you're about three hours too late because if you wanted to stop me talking to the police, you should have approached me before I went into the police station, not after. You've fucked it up and done it the wrong way around because I can't unsay things.'

'Do you think this is a joke?' Sunglasses asked. He was steaming now. 'I'm not here for a laugh, my friend. You have no idea who you're fucking with.'

'I'm not your friend and I know who I'm fucking with because I've just identified them at the station,' Lenny said. 'Let me give you a tip. I don't know if you've noticed but it's not sunny in here. In fact, it's not sunny outside either. Those Ray-Bans make you look like a right cunt.'

'Have you got a death wish?' Sunglasses asked, standing up. 'We'll fucking bury you.'

'You two mugs won't bury anyone,' Wally said, walking along the bench. Three other dealers were behind him. Two of them were taking pictures on their phones. 'I think it's time for you to fuck off.'

'You're a dead man,' Sunglasses growled.

'Walk away while you can still walk,' Wally threatened.

Lenny pointed his phone at the man and snapped a few pictures and then took some of the second man. He pressed record on the video feature.

'If those pictures go anywhere but on your phone, you're dead, understand?'

'Did you just threaten to kill me?' Lenny asked, recording the men. Sunglasses stooped closer and pointed his finger at Lenny but didn't say anything, his face turning red with anger. He turned and walked away. 'Is that it, are you going? You two are a fucking joke,'

Lenny said as both men walked away quickly. 'My friends at the Matrix unit will be made up with these photos. I bet they already know who you are. You can go and see your friends in prison. Prick!'

'Don't come back, dickheads,' one of the dealers called after them.

'See what car they're in, Lenny,' Wally said. 'Get the plate and I'll get you a name and address.'

The men walked away quickly. They reached the bottom of the steps and headed for the exit. Lenny followed them at a safe distance and filmed them climbing into a black Nissan. He took a few pictures of the reg plate and then went back into the saleroom. His hands were shaking when he turned the camera off. Whoever they were, they were amateurs or thick as fudge, but it didn't take a brain surgeon to pull a trigger. Any idiot can do that.

'What was that about?' Wally asked. The other dealers gathered around him.

'Have a guess,' Lenny said, shaking his head. 'I was at the police station this morning and they must have followed me.'

'Is this about who shot you?' one of the dealers asked. Lenny nodded. 'You need to be careful, mate. Do they know who did it?'

'They do now,' Lenny said. 'One of them lives in Dublin and the other two are inside. Those two were just jokers. Whoever sent them must be short of men.'

'That's because most of them are inside,' Wally said. 'Still, you don't need that kind of aggro when you're at work.' Lenny nodded and looked at his phone. 'Any more mither, just let me know.'

'Thanks, Wally,' Lenny said.

Lenny scrolled through his phonebook. He selected a number and pressed call. It was answered on the third ring.

'Lenny, that was quick. I wasn't expecting to hear from you so soon,' DCI Chrissie Dunn answered. She had given him her number and told him to call if there was anything at all bothering him. She sensed something was amiss. 'Are you okay?'

'I'm okay but I have a problem with two thugs trying to put the frighteners on me,' Lenny said.

'You're joking,' Chrissie sighed. 'Already. What happened?'

'I went straight from your place to the car auction at Tuebrook,' Lenny explained. He walked towards his car. 'They know that I was in the station this morning and they followed me from Speke.'

'What happened?'

'I was sitting in the saleroom and two men sat either side of me and called me a grass. They asked me if I have a death wish.'

'Do you know them?'

'No. But I have pictures of them, and I have their vehicle and registration plate.' Lenny sent the images in a message.

'Have you got them?'

'Yes. That's very helpful, thank you.'

'Fucking hell!' Lenny hissed.

'What is it?'

'They have slashed my tyres,' Lenny sighed. He walked around the Jag. 'All four of them. They're two-fifty a corner. It's going to cost me a grand to replace them.'

'Can you get them sorted today?' Chrissie asked. 'I can get someone to pick you up.'

'Yes. I can sort it. That's not a problem.'

'Are there any cameras there?'

'Hundreds,' Lenny said. 'Trust me, these two are jokers. They are from the bottom of the barrel. Thick as fuck.'

'I'm going to get this reg put out and bring them in,' Chrissie said. 'If you can ask the auction to check the CCTV, we'll lock them up for intimidation and making threats to kill. I'm sorry about this. I was hoping they would think better of bothering you.'

'My question is why they were following me,' Lenny asked. 'I didn't tell anyone that I was going to see you today, so who knew at your end?'

'Only DC Harris and I,' Chrissie said. 'Don't worry. I'll be asking that question.'

'I'm not going to put my family in danger, Chrissie,' Lenny said, sighing. 'I will take my chances with these mugs, but my family can't be brought into this.'

'I know. I know.' She paused. 'I'll lock them up. Trust me that they won't bother you again.'

'I trust you, but who sent them?' Lenny asked.

'We'll be asking them that question,' Chrissie said. 'Once we ID them, we'll know more about who they work for.'

'I need to order four tyres.'

'Leave it with me.'

'Call me when you have them in the cells, so I can relax.'

'Okay. Talk later.'

Chapter 11. Sam

SAM WAS DRIVING BACK to his flat, listening to the radio. He was feeling anxious about the news that a body had been found in a storage facility in Warrington. The news reader said that the police were linking it to a missing man from Huyton. It was no longer a missing person case, and the police now had a murder to investigate. There was no doubt that the investigation would ramp up and Sam had been involved. Anthony Head had drugged and raped his best friend on the day that she died. Angela Deacon was the mother of two children fathered by Barry Maddern and Maddern had wanted revenge. So had Sam. It seemed like the right thing to do at the time but with hindsight, he wasn't so sure.

Sam had catfished Anthony Head online, pretending to be a teenage girl, and lured him to his death. Barry Maddern and his crew had bundled him into the back of a van and done the rest. They had done the actual killing, although he didn't know for sure what had happened. Sam had nothing to do with that side of the abduction, but he was still a key player in a murder. The fact Sam had lured him to his death meant he was an accessory to murder at the very least, wasn't he?

It would be virtually impossible for the police to trace him via social media as all the communication were via Anthony's mobile accounts and he had used two different numbers. Even his wife couldn't have known what accounts he had and what profiles he had used but there are always crumbs that can be followed if they're spotted.

Sam knew the police must have searched his social media footprint when he went missing, but they wouldn't have found his conversations with the girl he went to meet the day he went missing. They were carried out under different profiles and Sam had used disappearing messages that delete after 24-hours. Even if they did stumble across them, there would be no indication that the profile was not who she said she was. Anthony would have been talking to several women at the same time because he was a sex pest.

Sam had been careful, but he was still terrified that the police would come for him. He was also struggling with the guilt. Every time he saw Sandra Head staring out of her window, it pained him. He had no sympathy for Anthony Head, he was a rapist, but he felt for his family.

When he reached his street, he saw a marked police interceptor parked on the kerb outside the Head residence. Next to it was a dark BMW with black alloys. A detective's vehicle. It looked to Sam like the police had gone to break the bad news that Anthony had been found. He parked across the road and looked towards the house. Sandra Head wasn't standing in the window, but the lights were on, blinds drawn. The silhouette of a man cast a shadow onto the blinds. He envisaged her sitting on the settee while detectives explained that the body they had found in Warrington was her husband, Anthony. He couldn't imagine the pain she must be feeling. The minute strand of hope she must have had that he might be alive, was now severed and all her hope died with it.

The reality would hit hard. Her husband was dead, just as everyone suspected. Just as she had suspected herself but couldn't actually admit until now. There would be so many questions and things to do; a funeral to arrange. Telling the wider family the dreadful news. They would all have questions. How did he die? Was he murdered? Did he suffer? Who do you think killed him? Why did they kill him? And on and on and on and on…the questions would echo through the rest of her lifetime and there would never be answers because the people who knew the answers would never tell. They couldn't tell, not ever.

Sam opened the door and got out, grabbing his shopping bag. The wind swirled around the car. He ducked his head against the freezing rain and jogged to the front door, his feet splashing in the puddles. The door had been left open again. Someone had left the lock on the latch, which meant anyone could walk into the hallway. No doubt it was the cuckoo in Les's flat. Sam stepped inside, closed the door, slid the snip and locked it.

'Leave that open,' a man said. His accent was strong. Sam turned to face him. It was the man he had seen earlier, still wearing a dark tracksuit and white trainers. 'I'm expecting some friends to call, and they haven't got keys.'

'It's getting dark, so the door needs to stay locked,' Sam said. 'The other residents in the block like it to be locked so that we know burglars can't just walk in. It's just common sense and common courtesy to the other residents but you don't actually live here, do you? Isn't it time you moved on?'

'Don't worry your little head about me and what I'm doing. I'll make sure no one just walks in. Think of me as security,' the man said. 'Go to your flat, lock your door, put your television on and mind you own fucking business and let me get on with mine.'

'Or what?' Sam asked. 'What exactly are you going to do?' Anger flickered in the man's eyes, but he looked uncertain of his next move. Being challenged wasn't in the script.

'Do you really need me to answer that?' the man asked, smiling. 'You don't want to step into that world, trust me. Do yourself a favour and don't push this. Leave the door unlocked and go upstairs to your flat. No one is going to burn the place down.'

'I don't think so,' Sam said. 'The door stays locked.'

'You're making a huge mistake.'

'So are you,' Sam replied. He gestured to the police car across the road. 'I see the police are across the road, talking to Sandra Head about her husband.'

'I have no idea who she is. So, what?'

'They found a body in a storage facility in Warrington. Her husband vanished and I heard on the radio that they think it's him that they've found.' The man looked out of the window at the police vehicles. Sam shrugged. 'I can see one uniformed vehicle and one unmarked, which will be murder detectives. It's probably a gang-related killing, which means the police will be on the estate, knocking on doors asking if we've noticed any gang-related activity lately.'

'Is that right?' the man asked, shifting nervously. He went to the front door and peered through the glass. 'The people in this block need to say that they've seen fuck all going on. Or is there a grass or two in the building?'

'Are you fucking stupid?' Sam asked, shaking his head. 'I'll be telling the Dibble exactly when you arrived and the names of the young lads who have been visiting you. So will the other neighbours in here. We want you gone.'

'I'll be telling them exactly the same thing, don't you worry, Sam,' a man said from upstairs. His name was Andy. He looked down over the banister rail at the cuckoo. 'You need to pack up and fuck off mate before the bizzies start knocking on doors. I know the names of all the youngsters going to see you. I will make sure the police know too.'

'I'll be telling them exactly the same thing,' a woman from the ground floor said, from her front door. 'I know most of those kids and their parents. Are you alright, Sam?'

'I'm fine, Mary,' Sam said. 'The door stays locked or those uniformed officers in that car are going to get a tipoff that there's a shitload of drugs in that flat, and that we suspect child exploitation is going on.'

'It looks like I'm surrounded by snitches. Child exploitation?' the man said, nodding. 'That's a heavy accusation.'

'We've all seen the young lads coming and going. New trainers in exchange for carrying stuff on their bikes for you?' Sam shrugged. 'That is exploitation.'

'You're a proper nosey parker, aren't you? Your card is marked, sunshine, and so are yours,' the man said to the other neighbours. 'You need to wind your neck in and keep your mouth shut unless you want your jaw wired up. You'll be sucking soup through a straw for a few months.'

'Eh, gobshite! We all heard you making threats. Do you think you're the big man, do you?' Mary said, pointing her finger. Mary was a sixty-six-year-old pocket battleship. 'Go and pack up your shite and do one out of our building. Take your druggie mates with you.'

'Wow, that's a bit aggressive. Go back into your flat and get on with your knitting, Mary,' the man said. 'This isn't a nice conversation for a frail old lady like you.'

'I might be a frail old lady, but my son is coming to visit tonight. He's not frail, and you better not be here when he gets here. His name is Tommy Young. Have you heard of him?' Mary asked. 'He's a bouncer in town. Works on all the big doors.'

'Tommy Young will fucking break you, mate,' Andy from upstairs added. 'I'd pay to watch that happen. Do me a favour mate and stay put so I can watch him destroy you.'

The man nodded and looked up at Andy. He made a gun with his fingers and pretended to fire it.

'Can Tommy stop a bullet?' He smiled. 'Remember that you were warned.' He glared at Sam and went inside the flat, closing the door. Sam waited a few seconds before he walked away. He didn't like the way that had ended.

'I didn't know you had a son, Mary,' Sam said, winking.

'Neither did I but it sounded good,' Mary said.

'And who the fuck is Tommy Young?' Sam whispered.

'Fuck knows,' Mary said. 'It was the first name that came into my head.'

'Nice one, Mary. Take it easy,' Sam said, kissing her on the cheek.

'You take care of yourself,' Mary said, hugging him. 'You're all skin and bones. You need a bit of meat putting on you. Are you eating properly?'

'I do alright. Are you offering to cook for me?' Sam asked.

'You can go to the chippy down the road if you want a good dinner,' Mary joked. 'My days of cooking for a man are long gone. I'll be going down there myself shortly if you want anything?'

'I've got chilli for tea. I'll see you later,' Sam said, heading for the stairs. When he reached the landing, Andy shook his hand and then went towards his flat. His youngest child was standing in the doorway.

'Hello Sam,' she waved.

'Hello Lucy. How's school?'

'Boring.'

'No change since I was there,' Sam joked.

'See you later,' Andy said, closing the door.

Sam heard the door to Les's flat open. He looked over the rail and watched the cuckoo walking out of building, a thick padded coat on, hood up, and a holdall in each hand. The door closed behind him and clicked shut. He turned and looked up at Sam through the glass. They locked eyes for a moment. There was venom in the cuckoo's glare. He grinned and Sam found it unnerving, but he didn't look away. The cuckoo turned and walked away, and Sam went down the stairs to make sure the door was latched. It was.

Sam climbed up to the landing and let himself into his flat. He switched on the heating to shift the chill that had settled into his bones. Switching on the lights and the television, he went into the kitchen and put his wine and milk into the fridge. There was a plastic tub of chilli left over from the day before and he took it out and put it into the microwave, ready to eat when he got hungry. The news was covering events in Ukraine.

Sam went into the living room and looked through the window. The lights were burning in the Head residence. He could see uniformed officers at the door. Sam was going to close the curtains when the window exploded into a thousand pieces, showering him with flying shards of glass. A brick hit him squarely in the face, breaking his nose and splitting his top lip. He fell backwards and cracked the back of his head on the edge of the coffee table. Blinding white lights flashed in his brain and then everything went dark.

Chapter 12. Police Station

he's takin' her time making' up the reasons, to justify all the hurt inside, guess she knows from the smiles and the look in their eyes...

DAVID ISLE WAS TAKEN into custody and put into an interview room to meet with a duty solicitor. He waited two hours, which felt like ten, and all the time he was panicking that they would send him to jail. Heather's ex-husband – technically they were still married – was in there and he wasn't best pleased that David was with his wife. He had sent threats via social media, which were very nasty and from what Heather had said about him, he would deliver on them.

The solicitor was Howell Jones, a criminal lawyer with a reputation for defending even the most difficult cases with aplomb. His reputation for being reasonable and polite was untarnished; even the police detectives liked him, despite the fact he was batting for the other side. He was reading the details of the incident at the Norris home, which was an unusual one. It's not often a parent is arrested for shooting a child in the face. David was sitting next to the wall and felt uncomfortable and penned in and he wanted to go home and smoke cigarettes. Howell Jones wasn't the friendliest of people and David felt like he was looking down his nose at him.

'Okay David, let me tell you the situation as I see it, and you can tell me if I've got anything wrong, so we're on the same page,' Howell said, looking over his glasses. His dark pinstriped suit was shiny at the elbows as if it had been worn for many years. Dandruff and grey hair spotted the shoulders. David put him in his sixties. 'You have moved into the home of Heather Norris, and she has four children with a different man, who is in prison at the moment?'

'Yes. Is that significant?' David asked. 'I mean that he's in prison.'

'Not really at this point. We're not here to discuss the merits of his ability to be a responsible parent while he's in prison as the children are safe in the care of their mother.' He raised his forefinger. 'Or so they should be.'

'Okay. I understand that and they are safe with Heather and me. We look after those children, no matter what social services say.'

'If you say so,' Howell muttered. 'The oldest girl, Hope, was walking to school when she was hit in the face with a pellet from an air rifle and she's subsequently in hospital?'

'Yes. But I didn't shoot her.'

'Let me get this straight. She had left the house and grounds and was walking on a pavement along a busy street?'

'Yes.'

'And how busy is the street?'

'At that time in the morning it's the school run and people are driving to work. It's chock-a-block.'

'And there are how many houses around yours. Roughly?'

'We live in a semi-detached,' David said, proudly. 'There are houses all around us, front and back.'

'I see. And they brought you in because you have an air rifle, which you keep in your wardrobe?'

'Yes.'

'Are you aware of any other neighbours who own airguns?' Howell asked.

'I hear them going off all the time. A few of the families at the back of us shoot bottles and jars as targets,' David said. 'You can hear the shot and then the glass smashing.'

'How many, roughly?'

'Four or five, at least.'

'What is the make and model of the airgun you own?' Howell asked.

'It's a Meteor .22.'

'Is it a powerful rifle?'

'Over short distances, yes. It's a target gun really,' David said. 'I used to shoot tin cans with it when I lived at my old place, but I hardly use it now because of the kids and the dog. I have to think about their safety, you see.'

'Of course. Would it put a hole in a tin can?'

'Yes. Definitely. Good for killing rats as well,' David bragged.

'I think you should not mention the tin cans or the rats.' Howell made some notes. 'The only reason they brought you in is because you own this gun?'

'That's pretty much it,' David said. 'It's all a big misunderstanding. The detective didn't like me from the off and the social worker who was there has got it in for me. I can tell he doesn't like me one bit. He's always got a shitty on and doesn't leave Heather alone. She hates the bloke and she's sure he's trying to remove her children, which might be a good thing, if I'm honest.'

'You think it would be a good thing if she has her children removed?' Howell asked, stunned by the comment.

'It would be a good thing for our relationship, they're a pain in the arse,' David said. Howell shook his head. 'It's no fun trying to bring up four kids on benefits. We have no social life or time for ourselves.'

'I think we should not mention your domestic situation at all,' Howell said.

'I agree. That social worker is a proper Hitler, telling us what we should do and what we can't do. He ordered a hair strand test last week to check if Heather is taking drugs, which she isn't. But I can tell by the way he looks at me that he doesn't like me. I think he's got it in for me.'

'I've met him several times. He's a senior social worker, with an excellent record and very experienced from what I can see. He's a professional going about his job. Why would you assume that he's got it in for you?' Howell asked, frowning.

'He has got a shitty attitude,' David said, oblivious to what he'd been told. 'I'm thinking of putting in a formal complaint against him, see how he likes that. He's a disgrace.'

'In my experience, being argumentative and making disparaging comments about professionals doesn't go down well in situations like this,' Howell said, lowering his voice. 'Be polite and cooperate, answer their questions honestly and keep your opinions to yourself. We'll have you out of here in a few hours. Okay?'

'Yes.' David folded his arms as if he'd been told off by a teacher. 'I'm just saying what I think.'

'It would be best not to say what you're thinking.'

'I can have an opinion.'

'Keep it to yourself. Don't make any unnecessary comments.'

'Okay,' David said, nodding. 'But I'm warning you that this policewoman doesn't like me. I can tell a mile away. You'll see what I mean.'

'Just be polite. Manners go a long way.'

'I'm just saying, that's all.'

The door opened and DI Jane Bennet walked in with another female detective. She put her laptop on the table and sat down. Her dark hair was tied up into a ponytail and smelled of White Linen. David thought she looked fit in her dark suit, slim and athletic. Unlike his partner Heather, who was bit saggy after having four children. Lots of women keep in shape after giving birth but Heather had let herself go. Not that he ever told her that. There was no harm in looking at other women and comparing them. Not in his book. He stared at her breasts.

'I'm DI Bennet, we met earlier, and this is DC Croft.' Croft was black and attractive. One thing David wasn't, was a racist. He would do her at the drop of a hat. He switched his gaze to her lips. DC Croft felt his eyes on her and she frowned her distaste. 'We're going to ask you some questions about what happened at the Norris home this morning.'

'Objection,' David interrupted.

'Pardon?'

'Objection. It's my home too,' David said. Jane looked at him to expand. 'I live there too.'

'You do. We're aware of that. We're not in an episode of crown court. There's no need to say, objection.'

'They do it on the telly. I'm just clarifying that it's my home too.'

'Okay, thanks for that.' Jane looked confused but continued. 'There was an altercation in the kitchen between you and Hope this morning?' Jane said. 'At breakfast.'

'Is that a statement or a question?' Howell asked.

'Both,' Jane said. 'I'll rephrase it for you. Was there an altercation between you and Hope in the kitchen this morning?'

'I wouldn't call it an altercation. We don't really get on,' David said, shaking his head. He wasn't sure what 'altercation' actually meant. 'Hope doesn't like me being there. I'm not her dad and she doesn't like me being with her mum. She can be difficult with me.'

'Can you answer the question please?' Jane asked.

'What was the question again?'

'Was there an altercation with Hope, this morning?'

'Let me explain. We wanted a cup of tea and the kids had used all the milk again. They do it all the time,' David said. 'I said something about them being greedy and she told me I'm not her dad and to fuck off.' He shrugged. 'It's not the first time she's told me to fuck off. She doesn't like me at all.'

'Yes, you've said that she doesn't like you,' Jane said. 'Did you call her a spoilt brat?'

'I can't remember, to be honest,' David lied. 'I might have done. They are spoil brats, all of them. Spoilt rotten. I say what I think. Some people don't like that, but it's best to be open and honest.'

'So, you did call her a spoilt brat?' Jane asked. David shrugged.

'Don't remember.'

'Did you threaten to give her 'a fucking good hiding' as Jacob recalls?'

'I don't remember saying that,' David said, shaking his head. 'That doesn't sound like something I would say.'

'Pru and Paige recall you saying exactly the same thing as Jacob does,' Jane pushed. 'You said, 'you should go to school before I give you what you deserve' and Hope asked you what she deserved, and you replied, 'a fucking good hiding'. Does that ring any bells?'

'No, not really. The twins would say that. They don't like me,' David said. 'There's a lot of jealousy because I'm with their mother.'

'All three of them distinctly recall you saying it,' Jane said. 'You threatened Hope with violence, shortly before she was shot in the head. You can see how it looks, David?'

'Looks can be deceiving, DI Bennet,' David said, nodding. 'You of all people should know that.' The detectives exchanged glances. 'Never judge a book by its cover.'

'How old are these children?' Howell asked, removing his glasses. He needed to move the conversation on.

'Jacob is eight and the twins are ten,' Jane said.

'Children are notoriously unreliable as witnesses,' Howell said. 'Let's get to the crux of the matter. Is there any evidence that my client actually fired his rifle at Hope Norris this morning, like an eyewitness?'

'No.'

'Then why is he here?'

'When he was asked if he owned an air rifle, he lied to the officer,' Jane said. 'Jacob overheard him and told me that, 'David had told a lie to the policeman.'' Howell nodded and looked at his client, but David didn't respond. 'Why did you lie about owning a gun, David?'

'Because you lot don't like me,' David said. 'I've been stitched up a few times over the years, people twisting stuff to suit themselves and to make me look guilty for things I haven't done. I thought it would be easier to just say no. The police have never treated me fairly. I must have one of those faces.'

'You lied because you think the police don't like you?'

'I lied because I didn't want to end up in a cell, waiting for you lot to make it look like I'm guilty.' David sat back and folded his arms. 'Why don't you just ask Heather if I took the gun from the wardrobe this morning. She was in bed at the time. She's not going to lie about it if I shot her daughter, is she?'

'I've met a lot of people who lie for their partners, David. It happens every day,' Jane said. 'Tell me what happened after the children left for school.'

'I got a pint of water and went back up to the bedroom,' David said. 'I made a bit of a joke about there being no kids around and we were having a bit of a kiss and cuddle when the kids burst back in, shouting about Hope being shot.'

'You didn't go to the window?'

'I might have done after the kids came back but not before,' David said.

'Unless you have a witness to the contrary, you don't have anything, DI Bennet. This is a fishing expedition, and you were hoping for a confession, but clearly, you're not going to get one,' Howell said, closing his laptop. 'I think we're done here. It's pointless dragging this out any longer. You can release my client immediately, if you would be so kind.'

'You can go for now,' Jane said. 'Don't leave the country.' She stood up and left the room. The door closed behind the detectives and David felt disappointed. He was beginning to enjoy watching the detectives struggling.

'Are you not going to say sorry or goodbye?' David said, feeling hard done to. 'I told you she doesn't like me.'

THAT EVENING

Jo Lilly was at home pouring a glass of Villa Maria, her favourite white wine. Her husband, Lenny, drank red wine which she thought was like vinegar, but he loved it. It had been another tough day at the office, some were worse than others, but they were all tough.

Jo was feeling anxious because Lenny had been to the police station that morning and she had been sick with worry all day. She wished it could just be forgotten about so they could get on with their lives, but the police were adamant that they needed to identify the men who had shot him. They had shot him because Jo had taken Angela Deacon's children into care when she died, and their father Barry Maddern was a psycho gangster. She had seen and heard some terrible things in her years in child protection, but the worst phone call she had ever received was the one telling her Lenny had been shot, and was in intensive care. The sense of sheer terror was unforgettable. When they had kissed and said goodbye that morning, she never for one moment thought that he might not come home. She had never been so frightened in her life.

Lenny was pretending he wasn't fazed by going to the police station, but she knew he was. The attack had traumatised him, but he refused to allow it to show, not even to her. She had seen him staring at the bullet wound in the mirror, his eyes glazed, deep in thought. When she asked him what he was thinking, he said it was better if she didn't know. An inch either side and he would have been dead, simple. Knowing that he had nearly died alone in an empty car park had changed him. The shooting had made him feel vulnerable and beneath the tough exterior, he was frightened of it happening again. The odds of surviving being shot on two occasions were millions to one. She could sense his anxiety; he was saying one thing but feeling another and keeping it to himself. He was feeling something completely alien to him, fear of being outside, around people, in the supermarket, at the petrol station, everywhere was dangerous.

Sensing what people were feeling had been part of her job for over a decade. Working in child protection meant talking to liars on a daily basis and being able to identify when they were lying and when they were just bending the truth. There were no absolutes, and reading people couldn't be taught overnight. It was a skill honed over years. Jo knew Lenny better than he knew himself and he was struggling beneath the surface, and he didn't like to struggle.

He hadn't called her from the auction, which was unusual. Jo had rung him three times and it had rung out and gone to answerphone. Something was wrong and he was avoiding talking to her, which was also unusual. He was overdue being home, and she checked her watch to see how late he was. Forty minutes. She dialled him again and he picked up.

'I'm here,' he called from the front door. 'Have you missed me?'

'Why haven't you been answering your phone?' Jo asked, worried. She kissed him on the cheek, and they hugged. 'Are you okay?'

'It's been an eventful day and I've been on the phone most of the afternoon. I needed four tyres on the Jag and no one had four, so I managed to get four from different suppliers. It's taken hours, sorry but I didn't want to worry you.'

'Not answering your phone worried me, Lenny,' Jo said. 'If you don't answer your phone, I think you're lying in a pool of blood for fuck's sake!' She hugged him tightly and kissed his forehead. 'Don't do that to me. Answer your phone.'

'I didn't want you to worry,' Lenny said. 'I thought telling you what had happened was worse. I didn't know what to say.'

'What are you talking about, what happened?'

'I don't know where to begin,' Lenny said. 'Sit down and I'll top up your wine.'

'I've got one.'

'You'll need another one,' Lenny said, taking her glass. 'I think you'd better let me fill up that glass. It's been a very difficult day and I suppose I had better start at the beginning.'

She didn't like the sound of what Lenny was saying. He sounded stressed and frightened, and that was unusual, to hear fear in his voice.

'When I set off from here this morning, everything was fine, and I wasn't too worried at all, but I was being followed.'

'Followed by who?'

'A couple of heavies, probably sent to see if I'm talking to the police.'

'And they followed you to the police station?' Jo asked. Lenny nodded. 'Tell me what happened when you got to the police station.' Jo followed him into the kitchen and watched him take a new bottle of Villa Maria from the wine fridge. He opened it and topped up her glass, before filling up a glass with rioja for himself. They chinked glasses and he kissed her lips gently.

'I met the chief inspector, who is a woman,' Lenny said. 'I was expecting a bloke. She took me through to the identification suite.'

'How did the identification go, was it as bad as you thought it was going to be?'

'The identification was the easy part of the day, if I'm honest. The DCI is called Chrissie Dunn, and she's a nice lady. She put me at ease, and we spent a few hours going through mug shots. I was losing the will to live, at one point. When you look at the faces, your brain tells you they're familiar, similar, and they might be someone you know. It's weird,' Lenny said, sipping his wine. 'Then an image came up on the screen, which I recognised.'

'Oh my God. Who was it?' Jo asked.

'It was the guy who shot me.' Lenny paused and sipped his wine. The impact on him was clear. 'It was the weirdest thing that I've ever done. Sitting there, looking at the face of the man who put a bullet in my belly was absolutely bizarre.'

'I bet it was bizarre. How awful for you. You had to see his face again,' Jo said, looking shocked. 'And did the detective know who he is?'

'Yes. He's a guy called Lewis Cashman and he's originally from Netherley but now he lives in Dublin.' Lenny paused and sipped his wine again. 'Look, Jo, there's no easy way to say this, so I'm just going to say it. Lewis Cashman is a hit man, and he was hired by Barry Maddern to find out where his children were. And then he was supposed to kill me. I wasn't meant to survive.'

'How do they know that?'

'Because that is what he does for a living. The police think they were disturbed by something, and they didn't check that I was dead. They thought I was dead.'

'I can't believe I'm listening to this,' Jo said. Tears were running down her cheeks. 'Are you telling me that the police actually know that this man is a hitman?'

'Yes.'

'And he's still out there on the streets allowed to walk around like nothing has happened.'

'Yes, that's exactly what I'm telling you, and I had the very same conversation with Chrissie Dunn, and she said, it's one thing knowing that he's a hitman and it's another being able to prove it in court. These things are much easier said than done.'

'Not from where I'm standing.'

'They have been trying to lock up Lewis Cashman for years, but witnesses disappear or just don't turn up in court. We all know how these things work. People get frightened, and they don't want to testify. I can't say I blame them, to be honest. I don't want to testify.'

'Okay, so you identified him, and they know who he is, so what are they going to do about it?'

'To cut a long story short, there is nothing that they can do about Louis Cashman at the moment.'

'I don't understand.'

'Because he lives in Dublin, which is southern Ireland, and it is out of their jurisdiction. He's untouchable while he stays there.'

'Is that the best that they can come up with?' Jo said, astonished. 'I'm afraid that is just not acceptable, and they need to do better than that. They can't leave a killer out there on the streets. What if he comes back and tries again?'

'Chrissie Dunn says that there is no way Cashman will try to leave Ireland, because he knows that he will be lifted as soon as he steps foot across the border. It's too dangerous for him to leave. There is more than one warrant out for his arrest. Interpol are after him too. He's a wanted man so he's safer over there.'

'I can't believe the police are telling you that there is nothing they can do about it. You were shot and nearly killed, and they know who did it,' Jo said, frustrated.

'It's an impossible situation and I can understand what she's saying, their hands are tied by jurisdiction.'

'No one knows more about jurisdiction than we do. We come up against it all the time. Once someone crosses a boundary, they can't be touched.'

'That's exactly what I'm telling you and I'm not happy with this situation either, but that is where we're at and there is nothing that we can do to change it,' Lenny said. He shrugged. 'On a brighter note, once they knew it was Lewis Cashman who had shot me, they showed me some more mug shots, and the two gorillas that were with him when they attacked me appeared on the screen.'

'You're joking,' Jo said.

'Nope. They were old pictures, but it was them. I identified them, and Chrissie knew who they were.'

'Really? She actually knows who they are?'

'Yes. They're called Mark Tyrer and Pete Jardine and they both worked for Barry Maddern for years. They are high up in the organisation.'

'Wow. I'm not sure if that is good or not but carry on.'

'The good news is they're inside, looking at money laundering charges. They have my statement, so they'll be interviewed for attempted murder. Chrissie says that they won't be getting out for twenty years.'

'Well, I suppose that is some good news, but I'm still not happy about this Cashman character being able to walk around and not worry about being arrested,' Jo said. 'It's not right.'

'Yes. I agree it is good news, but when I left the station, I was followed by two heavies who worked for Barry Maddern,' Lenny said, looking at Jo. She looked shocked. 'Before you start going on one, I don't want you to worry too much about it, and that's why I didn't answer the phone. I wasn't quite sure how to tell you what had happened without panicking you.'

'Will you please stop beating about the bush, and tell me exactly what happened,' Jo said, trying to remain calm. 'How do you know that you were followed from the police station?'

'Calm down, and I'll tell you what happened step by step.'

'This is as calm as it gets.'

'You don't look calm.'

'Lenny, I am calm. Tell me what happened.'

'Okay. When I got to the auction, I said hello to a few people that I've not seen for a while, and I bumped into Wally Jackson, who you have met before.'

'I think I remember him. Isn't he the guy with the jet-black hair, gold teeth and sovereign rings?'

'Yes. That's him. He looks like the type of guy you wouldn't buy a car from. You have just described Wally Jackson, exactly how he looked today.'

'Go on.'

'I went to the tea van and got a coffee and a cheeseburger from Della. She asked how you were and said to say hello to you. Everything was just how it used to be, and I was really enjoying being back in the swing of things.'

'It's been too long since you went to the auction. I know you've missed it.'

'I didn't realise how much I missed it, to be honest. Anyway, I went and sat on the top tier of the bench seats on my own, just so that I could chill and watch the auction go on. I wasn't really that bothered about buying anything, I just wanted to dip my toe in the water and see how I felt being in a crowded place again.' Lenny paused to take a drink of his red wine and think about his next words. Jo could see him recalling the incident, reliving it again. 'Two gorillas came into the sale room and sat next to me. They were like cartoon bouncers, an absolute joke to be honest.'

'It doesn't sound funny to me.'

'They sat either side of me. It was obvious they had come to intimidate me and find out what had been said at the police station.'

'Oh my God, you mean that they actually followed you all the way from Speke to the car auction, to put the frighteners on you in a public place?' Jo asked, astounded by their actions. 'How did they know you were going to talk to the police?'

'I don't know,' Lenny said. 'They may have been tipped off.'

'By the police?'

'They have people on their payroll.'

'I cannot believe these people walk around as if they are completely untouchable and think it's okay to threaten and bully people.'

'That's how they make their living.'

'What is wrong with these people and why are they still out there walking the streets?'

'I know it's difficult to understand but you know better than anyone the pressure that the police are under. They can't just lock people up because they are thugs.' Lenny shrugged and shook his head. 'Anyway, they told me that I must be a very stupid man for talking to the police and that their friends were not happy about it. They said I must have a death wish.'

'Did they threaten to kill you?'

'Not in so many words.'

'But they said that you must have a death wish,' Jo said. 'That amounts to the same thing in my book. Then what happened?'

'Wally Jackson and some of the other dealers had spotted that I was having bother, and they came and told the monkeys to do one before they got hurt.'

'Did they just walk away without doing anything?' Jo asked.

'They were being filmed on several mobile phones and some of the dealers had taken pictures of them. They must have realised that they were on a loser, and that the police would be involved if they didn't go,' Lenny explained, finishing his glass of wine and pouring a new one. 'I followed them to see what they were driving and to get a picture of their registration plate. You know how it works in our business. If we get a registration plate, then we can get a name and address quite quickly.'

'Yes, you can, but you know that that's illegal. I don't like you doing it but under these circumstances, I think that you were well within your rights to do that.'

'I called Chrissie Dunn immediately and told her that I had been followed from Speke to the car auction and that two gorillas had threatened me. While I was talking to her on the phone, I walked back to my car and found that all four of my tyres had been slashed.'

'The absolute bastards,' Jo said, angrily. 'Who do these people think that they are?'

'It's all part of intimidating a witness,' Lenny said.

'They think that they can just get away with anything and the reason for that is, nine times out of ten, they do get away with it!'

'They do get away with it and that's the problem,' Lenny said.

'Please tell me that the detective you were talking to has had these idiots arrested and locked up?'

'When I spoke to her, she told me that they would be locked up within a few hours and questioned for intimidating a witness and making threats to kill,' Lenny said, shrugging. The expression on his face said that there was a but coming. 'Wally Jackson ran the plates before I had even come off the phone to Chrissie Dunn. He said that they belonged to a Volkswagen camper, which was registered in Southport.'

'So, it was a dead end.'

'It took the police just over an hour to come up with the same information, so the long and short of it is, they don't know who the men are.'

'But you took pictures.'

'They were both wearing hats and one of them had sunglasses on, so their faces were covered enough to screw up facial recognition.'

'This is unbelievable,' Jo said, shaking her head. 'So, these thugs know that you have been to the police station to identify the men that shot you.'

'Yes.'

'And they are still out there driving around on false plates, and the police can't do a single thing about it.'

'Yes. That is the situation we're in and there isn't much that we can do about it except to be vigilant.'

'How do we do that?'

'We make sure we don't go anywhere that we can be isolated.'

'All this because I did my job.'

'I am sure the two jokers that came to me today are the very edge of the organisation.'

'What do you mean?'

'They were not subtle, and they were not clever. They're not serious players. If they were involved in any serious crime, they would be caught quickly, simply because they're stupid.'

'This is scary stuff, Lenny,' Jo said. 'What are we going to do about it?'

'We are very limited as to what we can do, but I do trust Chrissie. She said the police will do everything they can to make sure that we are safe.'

'We will have to hope that's enough.'

'In the meantime, I think we should order a Chinese and have another glass of wine or two.'

'How much did the tyres cost you?'

'Two hundred and fifty each for the tyres plus fifty pounds fitting, so it was just over the grand in total.'

'Ouch,' Jo said, kissing his cheek. 'I'll pay for the Chinese.'

Chapter 13. The Murder Squad

Come closer and see, see into the trees, Find the girl, While you can...

DCI FRENCH WAS HEADING up the Anthony Head murder investigation, which had started with an anonymous call made to Crimestoppers. The caller had told them there was a body in a freezer, in a storage unit in Warrington. It could have been a hoax, but it had to be investigated and they came up trumps. It wasn't going to be one of those cases that could never be solved; it was the opposite. All the pieces of the puzzle fitted together but some were still missing, so the picture wasn't complete.

Head was suspected of drugging and raping his next-door neighbour, who happened to be the mother of two children, and the father was a raging psychopath. She died later that day and Barry Mad Maddern had clearly ordered the hit on Head, and because Maddern was dead, there was no need to pursue it. They had no proof that Maddern committed the murder himself, but it was almost irrelevant.

However, someone had murdered Head, dismembered him and put the body into a freezer. If it wasn't for the tip off, it would have remained there until it could be disposed of, probably piece by piece. Whoever carried out the murder and disposal were as guilty as Maddern was. French and his team would need to follow the clues. The key was to trace whoever had rented the storage unit. The rent had been paid for two years in advance on a prepaid Mastercard, via a security company linked to Maddern. That fitted their theory that

Maddern had ordered the killing. One of the directors of the security company was Ged Tickle, who was in HMP Liverpool where he belonged. French had arranged for him to be interviewed about the unit by detectives Evans and Talbot. They had been to the prison that morning.

'Okay, tell me where you're at,' French said. 'How did it go with Tickle?'

'It was funny, to be honest. He was giving it all the hardcase nonsense that we usually get from him, but he looked like he was going to cry when we showed him the pictures of the unit.'

'I bet it came as a shock.'

'His eyes glazed over when he realised something was missing from it,' Talbot said. 'It looks like it was a trunk of some kind, and my guess is he put it there. His expression said it all without him saying a word. He was gutted, to say the least. Whoever took it from the unit hadn't told him that they were taking it.'

'You should have seen his face,' Evans said, smiling. 'I've never seen anyone so gutted in all my life. He was green. I thought he was going to puke.'

'What did he say about renting the storage facility?' French asked.

'Nothing,' Talbot said. 'He was adamant he didn't rent it, and he denies ever being there.'

'Of course, he did,' French said, nodding. 'What about knowing the victim?'

'Tickle says he doesn't know anyone called Anthony Head and that he had nothing to do with Angela Deacon when she was alive. He said he was aware Maddern had a couple of kids somewhere. He doesn't know anything about the murder of Anthony Head.'

'What do we think?' French asked.

'We think he knows about the unit, which means he knows about the body in the freezer. We need to get someone to point the finger and say, yes, he is the man who rented it,' Talbot said.

'Where are we with that?'

'We're going to interview the storage facility manager, Rupert Stokes,' Evans said. 'He's got guilty written all over his face. We have his bank details, and the techs are going through his accounts now. If we see any large amounts of money going in, we have him. We can use it to squeeze him to identify Tickle.'

'Good work but there's one more thing we need to look into,' French said. 'I want to know what was taken from that unit and who took it. Whoever took it, tipped us off, which means they wanted us to find the body and nail Ged Tickle for the murder. We need to identify who, in Maddern's crew, would benefit from him staying inside for life.'

'It's got to be someone near the top of the tree,' Talbot said. 'Stokes might be able to help us out with that one.'

'Go and get him and see what he has to say.'

Chapter 14. Mary

The girl was never there, it's always the same, I'm running towards nothing, Again and again and again and again...

MARY DENNIS PUT ON her winter coat and headscarf and took her shopping trolley from the storage cupboard by the front door. It was tartan with rubber wheels and a zip fastener; she had inherited it from her nan who went everywhere with it. She was still reeling from the events the night before and she hadn't slept properly. Poor Sam was still in the Royal recovering from his injuries, and she didn't think they would let him out anytime soon. He was hit in the face with a brick, which made a right mess of him and then he fell backwards and fractured his skull in the fall. The edge of the coffee table was hard and sharp and that's what did the damage to his head.

His face was a terrible mess, broken nose, split lips, and both eyes were black and swollen. He looked like he had been hit by a bus. The paramedics said he was lucky to be alive and Mary agreed with them. They said that if the neighbours had ignored the sound of breaking glass, he would have been lying there all night and could have bled to death. He probably wouldn't have made it until morning. When she went to his flat to see what was going on, it was such a terrible shock seeing him on the floor covered in blood and glass; he didn't have a clue where he was or what had happened. When she went upstairs, the police and Andy had broken the lock to gain access. They had to make sure he was okay because he wasn't answering the door. The large window at the front of his flat was shattered and the rain was blowing in. The housing association had boarded it up with wood this morning. It was like a scene from a horror movie. Sam was such a kind-hearted man, always had the time of day to say hello and see if she needed anything. Seeing him in so much pain had been heartbreaking and frightening.

There was no need to ask who had thrown the brick through the window. It was obvious. The police hadn't been much help. She knew the man had cuckooed the empty flat and that he had walked out of the building just before it happened but not much more than that. She had no name to give them and neither had any of the other residents. No one knew who he was. The police couldn't look for a man unless they had his name. They had looked at the empty flat, but it was locked, and they couldn't see anything untoward through the windows. They said they couldn't break in because there was no sign of any illegal activity, and the property belonged to the housing association. This was a massive problem with social housing on the biggest estates in most of the cities across the country. Mary had seen several documentaries that had been on the BBC recently about gangs and their county lines networks. It appeared that nobody was driving around on the streets with kilos of class A drugs in their vehicles. It was far easier to move their drugs around in small amounts using vulnerable teenagers as couriers. Like a paper round but with cocaine. The programmes that she had seen were calling it an epidemic and the cuckooing of properties was just another part of their process. That is what had happened downstairs in Les's flat. The dealers identified an empty property and set up shop, just like that. Obviously, they could close up shop just as quickly and move on. It happened just like she had seen on the telly.

No one had witnessed the brick being thrown through the window, so the police had nothing to go on, except a not very talkative victim. Sam wasn't saying anything. It was shocking that this had happened when the police were just across the road talking to the Head family, and that was another strange story. The man just vanished off the face of the Earth and then turned up in a freezer in Warrington. You couldn't write this stuff, Mary thought.

Whoever had thrown the brick clearly had no fear that the police were in the vicinity. They were across the road, but it didn't stop them hurting Sam. Mary recalled when she was a child, that they were terrified of adults. Teachers, parents, uncles, aunties, policemen, shopkeepers, were all figures of authority to be respected and feared. Respect your elders, they used to say but not anymore. This generation had no respect and no fear of anyone.

The sound of glass breaking had alerted the police to the fact that something had happened across the street but by the time they got there, the perpetrator was long gone and there were no witnesses around. They had asked Sam several times if he saw who had thrown it, but he had been very quiet. He was crying when they were taking him away but wasn't making any sense. He was obviously concussed by the blow to the back of his head. His face was so bruised and swollen, it didn't look like Sam at all.

Mary had known Sam since he moved into the block of flats as a young man straight out of the care system. He lacked in confidence back then and it was obvious that moving into his own property with the responsibility of paying the rent and bills was a daunting task for him. They often talked about things, and they were a comfort to each other. Mary had led a very full and colourful life and there weren't many situations that she hadn't come across herself, so giving Sam advice had been the most natural thing in the world. She had taken him under her wing, and they had a mutual affection for each other. She treasured their relationship.

Sam had no family to look after him, so she was going to see him at the hospital, and she would call at the shops to get some bits and pieces that she needed on the way home. She fancied a chippy tea, fish and mushy peas with lots of salt and vinegar. No chips because they gave her indigestion. There was a time when she could eat anything that she wanted to, and she would never put on an ounce of fat but as she got older, that had changed. Anything fatty before bedtime would keep her up all night. Sam would want her to go and see him, she knew he would. She could see his face lighting up when he saw her, eyes smiling but then the image changed to the bloody mess he'd been the night before. She tried to shake the thought from her mind, but it had shocked her.

Mary opened the door and stepped out of her flat and she had a sense of dread. Outside, the cold and wind and rain combined to make it an uncomfortable day. It was as if all the elements were telling her to stay at home today.

Don't go out today, there's more than a chill out there to worry about.

The hallway felt colder today, it wasn't heated. The housing association had disabled the communal heating to save money, but it felt even colder than usual. It was probably because Sam's window had been broken and the flat was open to the wind and rain all night. That was bound to affect the entire building. Of course, it would.

She locked up her flat and put on her gloves, heading for the communal door. It was still so grey and blustery outside, and the rain was running down the glass panels, which were misted with condensation. The headlights passing by were blurred, blobs of white and beige, the brake lights bright smudges of red. She wondered again if maybe she should stay in and keep warm and go to see Sam the next day, but she felt guilty leaving him in there on his own with no visitors. He would be feeling sore today and probably lonely and frightened. She couldn't leave him with no visitors. He was her friend and that's what friends do. They look after each other even when it's difficult.

Mary steadied herself and opened the front door and immediately felt the wind tugging at her clothes. It was cold and wet and off-putting.

Stay home.

She closed the door behind her and locked it, dragging her trolley as she went on her way. As she walked, ice-cold raindrops touched her cheeks; winter was entrenched now, and she longed for the warm summer days and light nights.

The bus stop was two hundred yards away and the bus was due in five minutes. She wouldn't have to wait long for it to arrive. Cars splashed by through surface water, lights on despite the early hour. It was one of those winter days where it never really gets light and then it's dark by four-thirty. Mary walked along the path to the pavement and then turned left to get the bus into town. It would take her to the main terminus behind Lord Street and then she would need to get another bus to reach the hospital. It would take an hour or so to complete the journey, then she might get a taxi back, but she couldn't afford to take one both ways.

Mary planned to buy some magazines, cordial and chocolate for Sam from the shops in the foyer. He loved car magazines and anything to do with motorbikes, although he had never owned one. One of the boys in the care home where he grew up had stolen a motorbike and he crashed while being chased by the police. He broke his neck and was a paraplegic until he developed sepsis and died. Sam said that he just liked to look at them and read about them but was too nervous to ride one.

She remembered the shops in the hospital had racks and racks of magazines of all types. There were all kinds of shops too; they were brilliant if you weren't the patient, she thought. They were handy for visitors to buy supplies for their relatives, but the patients would all rather be somewhere else than in hospital, no matter how good the shops were.

She knew more about hospitals than most people and they made her feel sad and alone. She had spent six months in the Royal Hospital when her husband was suffering from bowel cancer. The day they were told he had the disease was etched into in her mind like a date carved by a chisel into a headstone. He had been positive at first and fought through the rounds of chemo and radiotherapy like the strong man that he was, but it wouldn't go, and it ground him down. It had been a dreadful time, watching him fade away as the disease spread, first to his lungs, then his brain and his bones. There was nothing left of him when he died; he was a mere shadow of his former self. He had been a big fit man, strong as an ox, never smoked or took drugs but he was riddled with the disease at the end. Death was a release for him and a relief for her and she could never lose the guilt she felt after he died. She had spent the dark lonely hours in the middle of the night, praying for his suffering to end, for him to die. There was no hope for him, and he was in such terrible pain. She wanted it to be over for him and for her but when he passed, she was tortured by the guilt of what she had prayed for. Now she missed her partner of fifty-years like life itself.

They had run pubs for most of their lives and there were three-hundred mourners at his funeral. The day had gone by in a whirl of memories brought back by so many old familiar faces, friends and family, but when the funeral was over and all the well-wishers were gone, the emptiness left behind suffocated her. He had always been there for her, by her side night and day, her rock, and now life felt empty and pointless. She felt desolate without him. Her thoughts were always of him and the life they had shared together.

'Mary, Mary, your chin is hairy!'

A bicycle sloshed past her, splashing water from a puddle up her legs. She was startled by how close it had been to her. A hard splat hit the back of her head and she felt something cold running down her neck. She touched it and saw raw egg on her fingers.

'Do you think that's funny? You silly bugger!' she shouted. 'You could have knocked me over.'

'Mary, Mary, quite contrary, how does your garden grow?' a voice startled her. Another bike whizzed by her. The rider slapped her hard on the back of her head as he went by. Stars flashed in her mind. The blow stunned her.

'Mary, Mary, how does your lady garden grow?' one of them shouted.

'With silver bells and cockle shells,' another voice shouted. 'Do you still like a bit of cockle, Mary, you old dog?'

Mary stood still, frightened to move in case one of the bikes knocked her over. An electric scooter was riding directly towards her, swerving at the very last second. The man punched her in the shoulder as he went by. She cried out in pain. There was arthritis in the joint and white-hot pain flashed through her. She couldn't fathom what was happening to her.

'Help me!' Mary croaked but the wind carried away her cries for help, and no one heard her. She looked around for help, but the pavements were empty and there were no vehicles passing. The weather was keeping everyone in.

You should have stayed at home, in the warm, she thought.

'Leave me alone,' she cried.

'Mary, Mary, quite contrary. You've been a naughty girl, Mary.'

'What have I done?' Mary gasped. 'Why are you doing this to me?'

'You said you are going to grass, Mary,' one of the men said, slapping her face as he passed. Mary felt her cheek go numb and tasted blood in her mouth. 'We don't have grasses around here, Mary.'

Two young men on bikes circled her. Two more were on scooters. They were late teens, early twenties maybe, she thought. She couldn't move forward or backwards, and they rode around her, shouting her name. She was desperate for help, looking around to see if there was anyone there. One of them pushed her hard in the back. She staggered forward and fell onto her knees, scraping the skin. Her hands banged against the pavement painfully. The arthritis in her fingers screamed in agony. She felt tears of pain and frustration forming in her eyes, before they trickled down her cheeks.

'Oh, heavens above,' she gasped. 'Lord help me, please.'

'Mary, Mary, is this scary?' The man kicked her up the backside hard and she fell forward onto her face, scraping her chin on the concrete. Her teeth cracked together, and she felt one of them splinter. She spat it onto the floor in a globule of red goo. Saliva dribbled down her chin, speckled pink with her blood.

'Please make it stop,' Mary gasped. She felt blood running down her neck and she wiped her chin with the back of her hand, her skin smeared red. 'Why are you doing this? I'm an old woman. Someone please help me.'

'Mary, Mary, you snake in the grass, Mary, Mary, you've got a fat ass, Mary you're a fucking grass!'

'Leave me alone,' Mary pleaded. She started to sob uncontrollably as she got to her knees. Blood dripped into a puddle beneath her, red concentric rings spread across the surface. 'Please go away. Leave me alone.'

One of them kicked her shopping trolley and it clattered into the road, landing in the path of an Amazon van. It was crushed beneath the wheels and dragged down the road in a shower of sparks. The van skidded to a halt; its driver had no idea what he had hit. Mary watched the men circling her, hurling abuse. Disgusting things they were saying about her. She felt so weak and unable to defend herself. Fear chilled her to the bone. She was too frightened to speak or move. Her mouth opened but no words came out.

'You need to keep your gob shut, Mary,' one of the men said. 'Talking to the police will get you hurt.' He kicked at her, and the blow connected with her thigh. She screamed and there was an audible snap as her hip broke. The force of the blow knocked her backwards. She staggered and fell off the kerb onto the road and the double-decker bus that she was going to catch squealed to a halt just a yard away from her head.

The teenagers were gone before the bus driver could get out of his seat. An ambulance was called, and the paramedics assessed her. They suspected her hip was broken and possibly one of her wrists was fractured. Mary couldn't move because the pain was so intense. She thought about Sam and what had happened to him and now this. She was close to seventy and they had hurt her like this. Were they the same people? Did they have no morals or shame? The pain was incredible. The police arrived, called by the Amazon driver who had seen the men assaulting the old lady when he got out of the van. The police asked her questions, but she hardly heard them. Everything was just a blur.

'Did you see who assaulted you?' she heard someone ask.

'No one assaulted me,' she moaned. 'I fell.' 'Where is my handbag?' she whispered to no one.

'Has anyone seen her handbag?'

'Don't worry about your handbag for now, Mary. We'll find it and get it to you,' the paramedic said. 'We need to get you to the hospital.'

There was no sign of her handbag. The paramedics gave her morphine and put her onto a trolley. She didn't fancy fish and chips anymore, she thought as she drifted away.

Chapter 15. Andy

N*o, I can't forget tomorrow, when I think of all my sorrows, when I had you there but then I let you go..*

Andy Topper hadn't slept well and was tired, but he had to take Lucy to school on the way to work and there was no way around it. School was school and she couldn't miss it, no matter what happened. The school run was part of their daily routine as a family of two but today he wasn't feeling it; he wanted to turn over and sleep for a few hours more but there was no chance of that. The joys of being a parent.

The incident at Sam's the night before had disturbed him, and he couldn't relax enough to drop off to sleep and when he did, he had nightmares about men in tracksuits chasing him on bikes. The night before, when he had heard the glass smashing, he went straight to Sam's door and knocked on it, but Sam hadn't answered. He had run down the stairs and gone outside to see what had happened and the front window was gone. There was no one around.

The police had been across the road, heard the commotion and come to see what was going on. They approached Andy at first, suspicious that he was the culprit but when he explained who he was and why he was outside, they relaxed. Andy had told them he didn't know what had happened, but the glass was gone, and Sam wasn't answering his door. He said that he was concerned about his wellbeing. They had forced the lock and found Sam unconscious in his living room and called an ambulance. It took the paramedics twenty minutes to arrive on the scene which felt like an hour.

Suspecting this was a targeted attack, and not a random act of vandalism, the police had asked if anything untoward had happened and Andy gave them an abbreviated version of the angry conversation with the cuckoo earlier on. The police officers didn't seem surprised at all. They said they were aware the flat had been invaded and that it was part of a wider investigation, so they couldn't intervene before now. Apparently, it had been under surveillance for a few days, and they had been monitoring visitors coming and going. Andy thought it sounded like an excuse for not doing anything about it but didn't say as much.

Andy thought about the conversation between them and the cuckoo and regretted getting involved. Sam had stood up to the man, but they never worked alone. There were no lone wolves in the drug trade, there were always others further up the pyramid. The fact that Sam had been hurt badly worried him; it was an indication of what these people were like and how they responded to threats. It was on his mind all night and his dreams were haunted by images of Sam's bloody face. He felt that Lucy and himself could be in danger from a similar attack and that wasn't an acceptable situation. There was nothing he could do about it for now, but he thought about going to his parents' house for a few days until things blew over.

Lucy had been a handful at breakfast, but she often was. She didn't like going to school until she got there and then she loved every minute, coming home reciting everything that had happened, everything she had said, and everything she had done. She didn't shut up until teatime and beyond. But getting her there without a meltdown was a challenge some days. It was the thought of going that she didn't like, not the actual doing. Lucy could make a fuss about the most unimportant things and when she wanted something, she was like a dog with a bone; she wouldn't let it go and wouldn't listen to sense. Today was one of those days and Andy was too tired to be bothered where her favourite socks were.

Andy was a single dad and found it tough juggling bringing up Lucy and working a full-time job, but he did it well. He didn't know how people managed with more than one child, especially the lone parents on benefits. It wasn't easy with money but without was a nightmare he never wanted to experience, there was no mistaking that. He worked as a roofer and earned good money, so they didn't struggle that way. Lucy missed her mum, Paula, even though she had been four when she left them, and the sense of loss effected her behaviour. Paula was a heroin addict and couldn't give it up apart from the nine months when she was pregnant. Lucy was born clean, thank heavens, but the day after the birth, Paula went missing. They found her three hours later with a needle in her arm and she was back on it and was still on it as far as he was aware. The drug had her in its grip and always would have. Andy knew that Paula would never let the heroin go and the heroin would never let her go. They were entwined forever during her time on this planet.

Social services had become involved, and Paula had to leave the family, Andy had full PR. Lucy had contact with her mum at a contact centre at first, but Paula failed to attend so many times, it was destructive. When she turned up high, the contact stopped. Andy said Lucy could see her mum when she was older if she wanted to but until then, she was a liability and contact was stopped. He didn't want his child seeing her mother smashed off her tits or being let down, time after time. It would damage her eventually if it was allowed to continue and so they battled on through life together without her mother. Life goes on and the world keeps spinning even when someone wants to step off.

Being a single dad wasn't an issue, it was a privilege, although he did want to have a relationship with another woman one day. He had a few brief encounters, but they never went anywhere. It was difficult to commit and get sitters for Lucy at the weekend and they generally did something together anyway. If a new girlfriend wanted to see him at the weekend, Lucy would be there too. All the women he had dated thought he was looking for a mum for Lucy, which couldn't be further from the truth. No one else could be her mum, Andy was her mum and dad in one being. She wanted for nothing and needed no one else but him and their family. His parents were good to them with their money and their time. Her mum's parents were a waste of space and didn't bother apart from birthdays and Christmas. That suited him fine, and Lucy wasn't missing anything. She never mentioned them.

That morning, the trip to school was uneventful and the traffic wasn't too heavy, so they made it in good time. Lucy went to school in Roby, near the railway station, and Andy pulled in and parked up in the station car park. It was a pay and display, but he would only be a few minutes. He locked the van, and they walked hand in hand to the gate and Miss Pulmer smiled at him. She registered Lucy as present for school.

'Everything okay today?' she asked.

'We couldn't find her favourite socks, but she found her second-best pair, or we would still be at home.'

'Oh no,' Miss Pulmer said, frowning. 'They are very nice socks indeed. I have some just like them.'

'You're just saying that to shut me up,' Lucy said, smiling. 'Don't worry, I'm over it now.'

'That's good to hear,' Miss Pulmer said, smiling. 'Into the playground you go. See you soon,' she said to Andy as other parents arrived.

Andy thought Miss Pulmer was attractive but didn't want to put her in a compromising position by asking her out. She had smiling eyes, which seemed to light up when she saw him walking up the street. Dating parents wasn't ethical and it would be a breach of her contract if they started dating and were found out. He put any thoughts of a relationship out of his mind, kissed Lucy goodbye and walked back to the car.

The wind blew and he felt a shiver down his spine; it was colder every day now. Working on a roof in the winter was something only the hardiest of souls could cope with but it paid the bills and more. Dropping Lucy off had put his mind at rest for a moment. The school were good with her, and he knew she would be safe. The Sam incident was bothering him, and he couldn't shake the unease he was feeling. He should never have got involved in the altercation with the cuckoo. He was a drug dealer and they're not nice people. It was one thing being lippy with the cuckoo while there were other people around but what about when there weren't other people around? What about when it was just him and Lucy? You should have thought about that before you jumped in with both feet trying to make the cuckoo look like a twat, he thought.

He pictured Sam's ruined face and wondered, who looked like a twat now?

Lucy was in the playground talking to her new best friend Emma Critchley about the police being in their building the night before, and how her dad had helped them to break into their neighbour's flat because a brick had been thrown through his window. It was all so exciting. Emma was very impressed that a man had actually been carried out on a stretcher and put into an ambulance and that there had been blood. She was fascinated and said that she wished the police had been to their house, but it was always so boring. Nothing ever happened there. Lucy was milking the story about the ambulance man who had talked to her and asked her name and where she went to school, when her attention was caught by a man who came to the railings near them. He stopped and stared at the two girls.

'I know you. You're Andy's daughter. You must be Lucy,' the man said. He smiled and beckoned her to him. She shook her head.

'Come over here a minute, I've got something to ask you and I don't want everyone to know what it is.'

'I'm not supposed to speak to strangers,' Lucy said, shaking her head. 'I don't know who you are.'

'I'm a very good friend of Sam, the man who was hurt last night,' the man said. 'And I know your dad too. I saw your dad driving away and I waved at him, but he didn't see me. I want to know what happened to Sam last night, if you don't mind telling me.'

'Someone threw a brick through Sam's window, and it hurt his face.'

'Oh, that's horrible,' the man said.

'The police were there. He was taken to hospital in an ambulance,' Lucy said, she stepped a little closer. 'There was blood and everything.'

'Oh no!' the man said, shaking his head. 'That's terrible news. I hope he's alright. Come closer so you can tell me about it. Don't be frightened, I'm a little deaf in one eye,' he said, smiling.

'You can't be deaf in your eye,' Lucy said, laughing. 'You can only be deaf in your ears!'

'You're a clever girl,' the man said. 'Your dad, Andy said you were a super smart kid.'

'How do you know my dad?'

'We went to school together,' the man said. 'Just like you are now. I'm Jim.'

'Hello Jim.'

'And who is your friend?' Jim asked.

'This is Emma.'

'Hello Emma.'

'I think we should go now,' Emma said. She didn't like Jim. 'We shouldn't be talking to him. He's a stranger and remember, stranger danger.'

'I'm not really a stranger. I know Sam and your dad.'

'But we don't know you and sometimes bad men pretend to be someone else, so they can trick little kids.'

'Wait a minute,' Jim said. He took out his phone. 'I'm going to call your dad. Wait and say hello. He'll be so surprised that you're here.' He dialled a number. 'I can't wait to tell him that I met you. He will be so surprised.'

Andy was driving when his phone rang. The number was withheld. He answered it on handsfree.

'Hello.'

'Andy, say hello to your Lucy,' a voice said. 'Say hello to your dad, Lucy.'

'Who the fuck is this?' Andy felt his guts cramp.

'Hello dad!' he heard Lucy shout from a distance away. She wasn't close to the phone. 'I'm talking to your friend Jim.'

'Who is this?' Andy asked, his stomach in knots. This was bad. Very bad. 'How did you get this number?'

'You can call me Jim and getting your number was no problem. What you need to be concerned about is that I'm talking to your daughter in the playground at her school. She's a pretty little thing and it would be a terrible shame if anything happened to her, wouldn't it, Andy?' the voice said. 'Bad shit happens all the time to little kids. You can't watch them twenty-four-seven, you see. They are so vulnerable, and they break easily.'

'Who the fuck is this?' Andy slammed on his brakes and turned the van around in a U-turn, nearly wiping out a motorcyclist and almost hitting a lorry. Horns blared but he was oblivious. He sped away in the direction of the school. 'If you touch my daughter, I'll fucking kill you. Are you listening to me?'

'Hello dad,' Lucy spoke on the phone. She was right next to it now. 'Jim has picked me up and lifted me over the fence and I'm really scared, dad.' The call ended.

Chapter 16. The Hospital

You're gonna catch a cold, from the ice inside your soul, so don't come back for me, who do you think you are?

PHIL MOULT WAS TIRED of sitting in the relatives' room listening to Heather Norris ranting. She was blaming everyone but herself for the situation she found her family in. Her voice was echoing around his head, and he needed to get away from her for a while. The uniformed police officers were equally irritated by her constant waffling. The woman was a balloon who floated through life bumping into things with nothing of substance inside her.

Phil walked to the surgical ward just as a surgeon was walking out. He stopped and shook his head. Phil felt his stomach sink.

'How is Hope?' he asked.

'Not good. Removing the pellet was simple enough but we have no idea how hard the projectile hit her skull. The damage could be deeper than we thought,' the surgeon said, lowering his voice. 'The impact of the pellet has caused a lot of damage to the soft tissue and vascular system beneath the skull. She's been bleeding inside and that's caused pressure, which has caused more damage. We have stopped the bleeding that we can see but there will be bleeding in there that we can't see, so deep that we can't reach it. Her skull has been removed here,' he said, pointing to his head above his temple, 'so we could see the bleed and to release the pressure. We have no idea how much damage has been done or what the lasting effects might be, if she survives this.'

'If she survives?' Phil asked, his voice a whisper. 'Is she that bad?'

'I'm afraid so,' the surgeon said. 'She's in an induced coma for now and if she makes it through the next forty-eight hours, she has a chance, but it's fifty-fifty.'

'Can her mother see her?' Phil asked. The surgeon thought about his answer. 'She will ask me when I get back to the relatives' room.'

'She's in a very vulnerable state, her skull is still open,' the surgeon said, shaking his head. 'She can see her through the window, but it must be quick and there can be no noise on that ward, understand?' Phil looked unsure. 'All the patients in that particular ward need silence. If you think the mother might have a meltdown or become hysterical, then don't take her there. Keep her away until we can move her from critical care.'

'Okay,' Phil said. 'Thank you. You have my number if anything changes.'

'We have it in the case notes.'

'Thank you,' Phil said.

Phil took his time walking back to the relatives' room. He bought a cup of coffee, which tasted of water, and went outside for some fresh air. He had some decisions to make and none of them were easy. Heather was a firework, likely to go off at any time. He couldn't take her to the critical care unit. If she kicked off in there, she could do some damage. The police wanted to talk to her about David Isle and his role in the incident, so it might be best to get her to the station. She was saying that he didn't take his gun out of the wardrobe, in which case Hope had been hit by a stray pellet fired by a neighbour. It couldn't have been someone in a passing vehicle because the pellet struck the wrong side of her head for it to have come from the road. The pellet was fired from one of the properties to her right, either her own house or a neighbouring one. Whatever the outcome was, Heather needed to make a statement, but she was highly unlikely to want to leave the hospital while Hope was still in danger. What mother would be prepared to leave their child in critical care, he thought? The type of mother who stayed in bed while her children were hungry. The type of mother who didn't get out of bed to get her children ready for school. The type of mother who had four children and no food in the kitchen cupboards or money in the electric and gas meters but could buy cigarettes and weed. She was hardly mother of the century.

He had to put his personal opinions aside every day of his working life, even if it wasn't always easy to do so. What he thought didn't matter. There were rules to follow and processes in place to help them reach the best outcome for each family and each family was unique. Heather Norris and her new boyfriend were sailing close to the wind, and he had to question her capacity to realise how close she was to losing her children. Keeping them together for today was going to be difficult and there were arguments for both removal and for remaining at home. What the police uncovered was going to be the deciding factor, regardless of what common sense suggested. If they decided there was no evidence that David had removed his airgun and shot Hope in the face, then everything was reset to how it was this morning before they left for school. The kids were on a Child Protection (CP) plan but were still in the custody of their mother while their safety wasn't in question.

Phil took a deep breath and threw the coffee into the gutter before walking back inside. He reached the relatives' room and could hear Heather chunnering about how hungry she was and that not feeding her was against her human rights. A dog wouldn't be treated as badly as she had been. He paused before entering and braced himself for the onslaught.

'Oh, here he is, useless twat,' Heather said. 'You're supposed to be acting in the best interest of me and my children. How can keeping me in here be in my best interests?'

'Hope is out of theatre and she's in the critical care unit,' Phil said. Heather stopped talking for a second. 'She's very poorly and her skull is still open to relieve the pressure inside her skull.'

'I want to see her,' Heather said, bursting into tears. 'I want to see my little girl, right now!'

'You can't see her because she's vulnerable to infection because her skull is still open.'

'Fuck off, Phil!' Heather screamed. 'I hate you, you fucking cunt!' She lunged for him, and the officers grabbed her and restrained her. 'Get off me! I want to see my child, right now!'

'The critical care unit is a silent area, no noise at all and certainly no screaming and shouting. The surgeon will not allow you to go inside those wards. He cannot risk you losing it like this.'

'Fuck you, Phil!' She spat towards him, but the phlegm fell short of the target. 'I think DI Bennet wants her down at the station. There's no point in keeping her in here and she can't see Hope, so let's get it over with.'

'Don't you try and take me away from this hospital while my little girl is in critical care,' Heather shouted. 'What kind of person would think about doing that?'

'The type of person that wants a mother to go home and be with their children when they get home from school,' Phil said. 'I know you might think that I don't have your best interest at heart, Heather, but I do. And I certainly have the best interests of your other three children at heart and I want you to be there when they get home from school, not David Isle.' Phil shrugged and opened the door. 'If the police have finished interviewing him and let him go, then he'll go straight home and the last person that the twins and Jacob will want to see when they get home is David.'

'He's my partner, so you just have to get used to it.'

'It doesn't matter what I think of him, your children don't like him, and they will want to know what has happened to Hope from you,' Phil said.

'I don't know why you have to be such a twat all the time, Phil. What has David ever done to you to make you hate him so much?'

'That is where you are making a mistake, Heather, because I don't care one way or the other about David. I am there to look after you and your children and to make sure that you have the best possible chance to stay together as a family. If that is with David, then that's fine by me. If that means it's without David then that's also fine by me as long as those children are not in any harm and they are fed, clean and warm.'

'Listen to me, Phil, please don't let them take me away from this hospital until I have seen Hope and I know that she's going to be okay,' Heather pleaded. 'You must be able to see that I am not asking too much just to see my daughter.' Heather started crying and sobbing, her hands shaking. 'What if she doesn't make it and I haven't even had the chance to see her?'

'Hope has made it through the surgery and that is the most important part of the process, but they have put her into an induced coma because of the swelling on the brain. She will sleep now until they think that it's safe to wake her up. In the meantime, you could have been down to the police station, answered their questions, made a statement and be home in time to make your other children their tea.'

'Please Phil, let me see her.'

'It's not up to me whether you can see her or not. I've asked the surgeon if it would be possible, and he told me that if there's a possibility that you might have a meltdown and start screaming and shouting like you are now, then you must not be allowed anywhere near the critical care units. That is the advice of the professional in charge of the critically injured in this hospital and I'm not going to go against his wishes, no matter how difficult it is for you to leave Hope here. You have to trust me that she's in the best hands.'

'You're a bastard, Phil and you ponce around as if you are holier than thou and you think you walk on water but you're nothing but a jumped-up pen pusher who doesn't really give a shit about the parents that you deal with. You just check the boxes and write the reports and then you fuck home and forget all about the real people that you leave behind.' Heather folded her arms. 'I shouldn't have said that.' She took a deep breath. 'I know you care about my kids and they like you. And I know that you think that I don't care about my kids, but you're wrong. I do. Please let me see my child just for one minute.'

'I think it's pointless continuing this conversation while you are in that frame of mind. I know that you are upset but I am thinking about Pru, Paige and Jacob and how they are going to feel when they get home. They are going to want to see your face.'

'I'm begging you and I promise I will be quiet,' Heather said. 'I swear on my life that I will not make a sound. Please Phil, she's my child and no matter what you think, I love her.'

Phil could see the steely look in her eyes. His heart overruled his head, and he couldn't stop a mother from seeing a child who might not make it through the night.

'Five minutes and you will only be able to see her through the glass.' Phil beckoned her through the door. 'Come on, quickly.'

Phil turned to the police officers and gestured to the other door. 'I'll take her up to the critical care unit and then I think it will be best if you take her to the station and let her speak to DI Bennett and get that part of the investigation over and done with and then she can go home to her kids, hopefully.'

Chapter 17. Rupert

I work all night, I work all day to pay the bills I have to pay, ain't it sad? And still there never seems to be a single penny left for me...

DETECTIVES TALBOT AND Evans had been waiting for vital information from the forensic financial department, who were looking into the bank details of employees from the Storage King facility in Warrington. It had been more difficult than first anticipated because of the number of staff that had been turned over in recent months. Over 30 employees had come and gone in the last 12 months, but the number was fewer during the time scale they were looking at. Most of the accounts that they had investigated showed nothing unusual at all at first glance. The site manager, Rupert Stokes, had a Barclay's account, which looked unremarkable as well, until a second pair of eyes went over his bank statements. The first investigator who had looked at his account, was looking purely and simply for any large amounts of money being paid into the account; there were none. The second investigator analysed how much money had been paid into his account monthly and if it balanced with how much money was going out on a regular basis. The first investigator didn't look for months where the activity was much lower than the previous months, or the months after.

When the report came in and Talbot read it, he could feel the excitement burning in his chest. There was a period where Stokes had hardly used his account at all. The standing charges and direct debits were paid as normal. His wages had gone in at the beginning of the month and then at the beginning of the following month. There was nothing untoward with that, but he hadn't made any withdrawals from a cash machine or used his debit card for three months, so his balance had grown.

At first glance it didn't look to be criminal but when they analysed the figures, the only way that could have happened was if Stokes was using cash to buy everything. That meant that he had been in receipt of a large amount of cash, which he had spent over a period of three to four months. Unless he had a reasonable explanation for coming into such an amount of cash then he had some questions to answer. The receipt of any amount of cash had to be scrutinised nowadays, money laundering was rife, and the main reason organised crime gangs get caught, is because they're not clever with their money. If you can't explain where your money has come from, then you are going to have a problem with the police. It was that simple. The proceeds of crime are a massive signpost pointing at the criminal. Follow the money and find the culprit.

Talbot and Evans were on their way to meet Rupert Stokes at his home, which was in Widnes. Stokes had been reluctant to meet at his home, but Talbot insisted as he wanted to see what his house was like inside. If the place was full of high-quality items which probably couldn't be afforded on his salary or there was a Porsche on the driveway, then he would need to explain where the cash came from. If he couldn't explain where it had come from, they would probably be conducting the rest of the interview at the station under caution.

Their investigation needed to identify who had rented the unit and put the fridge freezer and the other item, which was now missing, into the room, and locked the door. The renter was involved in the disposal of a body at the very minimum. Stokes was the obvious candidate for their investigation to focus on. He was the manager, so he oversaw the operation. If people entered the facility to access their units, then it was policy to record the date and time and who it was that had accessed the facility. It was a simple code of practise followed by storage facilities all over the country and it was applied to stop people hiding the contents of crime, anonymously.

When Talbot reached the estate where Stokes lived, he slowed the car to a crawl and checked the numbers on the houses until he found the one he was looking for. It was on the left-hand side, and it was number six.

'That's it,' Talbot said. 'The one with the blue door.'

'There's no car on the driveway,' Evans pointed out. 'He agreed the time?'

'Yes.'

Talbot pulled to a stop and they got out of the vehicle. They looked at the house and all the curtains and blinds were open, and there was steam coming out of a flue at the side of the house, which meant the central heating was on. The detectives walked down the driveway to the front door and looked around. Across the road was a social club, which used to be a British Legion, and next to it was a sandwich shop and a barber. Talbot knocked on the door three times while Evans peered in the front window to see what was going on inside. Everything looked clean and tidy apart from a single coffee cup which had been left on the table in the middle of the room; next to it was a small plate with half a pie on it. A bottle of HP sauce was next to them.

'I don't think he's here,' Evans said. 'I'm going to take a look around the back of the house. You stay here in case he opens the door.'

Evans followed the path to the side of the house and then walked down a narrow ginnel between the neighbouring buildings. There was a wooden gate at the end. There was a hoop and clasp, and a broken padlock hanging from it. There was a scratch on the metal which looked shiny and new. He tried the latch to see if it was unlocked. It opened and he stepped through into the back garden.

Three wheelie bins were lined up against the wall. There was a greenhouse in one corner and a potting shed in the other. The lawn needed cutting and the grass was covered in fallen leaves. A rose tree had grown over the fence from the house next door, hanging bare and forlorn, waving back and to in the wind. The remnants of red roses were withered at the end of the branches, clinging on until the very last moment when they fell to the ground, where they would rot and become something else. Evans went to the back of the house and peered in through a set of patio windows. There was no movement inside and nothing looked out of place. He walked further along the house to the back door and was surprised to see that it was standing open. There was a pool of blood just inside the door on the kitchen tiles and blood splatter on the door frame but there was no sign of Rupert Stokes.

Chapter 18. Carla

Because of you, I never stray too far from the sidewalk…

SAM WAS SITTING IN the X-ray department waiting for a scan which was going to determine how bad the fracture to his skull was, whether his nose was broken or not, not that it mattered one way or the other. It was painful either way and it could not be put it in a cast, and it was hardly going to spoil his modelling career. The night before had been strange to say the least and he had foggy memories of what had happened at the flat, in the ambulance, and at the hospital. The cocktail of painkillers and antibiotics that he'd been given on arrival had made his head feel like it was full of candy floss. He couldn't think straight, and he wasn't sure if his memories were in fact memories or drug-fuelled dreams.

One thing was very clear in his mind and that was that cuckoo had claimed his retribution for Sam standing up to him earlier on that night. He didn't see the cuckoo throw the brick, but he knew he was responsible for it. Whether he had thrown it himself or had one of his lackeys do it, really didn't matter. The deed had been done. The message had been sent and it had been received and understood.

There was no way Sam and the other residents could tackle the likes of the cuckoo and his associates. It simply wasn't worth the hassle and when push came to shove, exactly what did they think they were going to achieve anyway? The answer to that was simple, absolutely nothing. The cuckoo had left the building that night with two holdalls and locked the door behind him, but that didn't mean that he wouldn't be back. Only now the circumstances were completely different. Before he left the area, the cuckoo had drawn a line in the sand, and he was daring people to cross it. Cross the line and see what happens to you and if you're not sure, then ask Sam because he knows the answer for certain.

As disappointing as it was, it's important in life to know when you're beaten, to know when there is no point in putting yourself in danger just to prove a point of principle. Sam had demanded that the door remain locked simply because he didn't want to back down and leave it open, so that the cuckoo's customers and couriers could come and go as they pleased. But in the cold light of day, nothing had been achieved. People would still be buying and selling drugs on the estate, and they always will be if they were available.

The police had been trying to stamp it out for decades and got nowhere. The prisons were full of people involved in the sale and trafficking of narcotics because it is one of the biggest businesses on the planet and there are billions of pounds being made daily. Governments and law enforcement agencies across the world were engaged in a constant battle to stop these organised criminals from selling their wares on the streets, just like they were in every city, on every continent.

And how is the battle working out for them? Sam asked himself. The answer is that they're losing, and there is no way that they can win. So, what chance did Sam have of stopping the cuckoo from selling his drugs in their building? The answer to that is no chance. He knew that before he had made the stand at the front door. It was a ridiculous sense of pride and a streak of stubbornness which had brought him to stand his ground. His reward was a house brick in the face. Well done Sam you clown, he thought.

Sam had his X-ray and the porter chatted endlessly about how amazing Liverpool Football Club was and how terrible the blue team were. On any other day it would have been amusing to listen to his anecdotes about his episodes following the reds home and away for 20 years. While his loyalty was admirable and his exploits funny, Sam was not really in the mood for an in-depth conversation. He was finding it difficult to concentrate on anything but the events of the previous night. If he had a time machine, he would go back to the day before and leave the fucking door open. And what harm would that have done? None. Idiot.

The porter took Sam to the ward and parked his chair next to the nurses' station, while he chatted and joked with the nurses who were about to change shift; some were just arriving and some ready to go home. On any other day it would have been nice to listen to the pleasant exchange that was taking place between workmates who do an amazing job under tough conditions, but today wasn't the day and Sam just wanted to get back in his bed.

Visiting hours had just begun and a steady stream of the patients' families and friends were arriving on the ward bearing gifts of drinks and edible food to supplement the slop that the hospital provided. Sam was pushed to his bed, and he felt the gaze of several of the visitors on him. They were looking at his broken nose and black eyes just a little bit too long.

'Hey mate, what does the other fellah look like?' one of the visitors asked, laughing at his own joke. Sam smiled and nodded and got into bed, not able to think of a witty reply.

It made him feel very embarrassed and uncomfortable, but he had nobody to blame but himself. He made a pact in his head that if the same situation arose in the future, he would look the other way and mind his own business. He had been told to go to his flat and mind his own business in the first place, but he hadn't listened. Sam took a drink from his bedside table and sipped it through a straw because his lips were too sore and swollen to drink directly from the cup. Knobhead.

'Your face is a right mess, mate,' a young girl said, approaching his bed, chewing gum. She was early teens at best, sporting a very smart white Armani tracksuit and white Nike Air Force One trainers. She was wearing a gold belcher chain around her neck and a bracelet to match. 'Is your nose actually broken, because it looks like it is?'

'I'm waiting for the x-ray results,' Sam said, humouring the girl, whoever she was.

'My mate Billy had his nose broken at the chip shop because he didn't pay for his weed on time. His eyes went black just like yours. I bet it's sore, isn't it, mate?'

'Yes. It's sore,' Sam said. He was hoping she would fuck off to whoever she was visiting but she sat down on the chair next to his bed and looked around the ward at the other patients. Sam wasn't sure exactly what was happening, but he knew that it wasn't good. Unless this girl was visiting another patient on the ward and was just intrigued by his injuries to the point where she felt the need to go and chat to him, then there was no reason for this teenager to be here except mischief.

'Who are you?' Sam asked the girl, not really wanting to know the answer. She looked at him and smiled but didn't stop chewing her gum.

'I'm Carla and you're Sam.'

'I don't know who you are, and I've never seen you before, so you've obviously been sent here by someone.'

'I have been sent here to give you a message and see how bad your injuries are,' Carla said, clicking a picture on her phone. She took several more pictures. 'People are very excited to see these,' she said, taking some more and sending them in a message.

'I'm really not up to playing games,' Sam said, getting annoyed. 'Can you stop taking pictures please.'

'I do as I'm told, so one more,' Carla laughed, taking another.

'Why don't you say what you've got to say and then you can go and leave me in peace?'

'I'm Carla Samson and I live in the next street to you,' she said. 'You probably know my brother, Jerry. He's hard as fuck. Everyone knows him. He was in the Paras for six years.'

'I can't say I've met him.'

'Jerry said that you'd had a bit of a run in with one of our friends, Frankie Wills, yesterday and he put you straight?' Carla said, moving closer to his bed. 'Listen to me, Sam. Jerry said that Frankie and his friends are bad news, and they all work for a guy they call Boothy. Have you heard of him?'

'Yes,' Sam said, nodding. 'He worked for Barry Maddern.'

'Not anymore. He's top dog now and he's a lunatic. He's stamping down on anyone who steps out of line, and you have pissed him off. You don't want Boothy and Frankie on your back, trust me.'

'I don't want to be involved with anyone like that,' Sam said. 'I just want to go about my business in peace.'

'Well, you're going the wrong way about it, Sam.' Carla lowered her voice. 'Like I said before, the guy you had a go at is Boothy's man, Frankie Wills. He's a proper bastard. You crossed the wrong bloke there, mate.'

'I did get into an argument with the guy, Frankie you said?' Sam asked. His head was spinning but this girl seemed to be okay. She was being sympathetic at least. 'He was squatting in the flat underneath mine. He cuckooed it and I was pissed off with the noise and said some stuff I shouldn't have, and it went a little bit too far and got heated. I wasn't thinking straight.'

'I get where you're coming from but it's better not to confront these guys. They're off their nut most of the time and they don't care who gets hurt. It's all part of the business to them. Anyone who stands up to them gets squashed, and I mean splattered,' she said. She gestured to his face. 'You got off lightly from some of the beatings I've seen them dish out.'

'It doesn't feel like I've got off lightly,' Sam shrugged. 'It looks like I've overstepped the mark and that's how I've ended up in here. If I could turn the clocks back, I wouldn't have had the argument in the first place. It was a mistake.'

'Fair play to you mate, at least you know the score. It's best not to argue with them as there is only ever one winner. I used to argue with them all the time at first, but it didn't get me anywhere so now I just do as I'm told. My brother has me going here, there and everywhere carrying who knows what, but he looks after me, so I go with the flow.'

'I think that's probably the best thing that you could do, especially at your age. There's no point in banging heads with these people. As you said there's only one winner. I hope your brother and Frankie and his friends are prepared to let this be an end to it. I'm prepared to apologise for what I said if that helps?'

'I will tell him what you said and I'm sure he'll be more than happy to put the matter to bed once you've paid him the money that you owe him,' Carla said smiling. Sam felt his stomach drop though the floor. He didn't reply because he couldn't think of anything to say. The last thing he wanted to do was dig himself into an even deeper hole than he was in already.

'I can see that you're confused by that but because there were so many Dibbles around at your flat last night, Frankie wasn't able to conduct his business as usual, so you owe him the money that he would have made last night. And he said that he needs to be paid before the end of the week, which is Sunday.'

'I can see what Frankie is saying and I understand why he is annoyed by what happened, but I don't have a lot of money and I'm not sure why he thinks I'm responsible for the money that he lost last night,' Sam said. 'After all it was him that threw the brick.'

He knew in his heart of hearts that he was wasting his breath. This was just another message to say don't ever fuck with me. It said we are in charge, and you need to do as you're told and keep your mouth shut. It was a power play, and it was a good one, saying you're in a hospital bed but this still isn't over, dickhead. He was daring someone to challenge him again and face the consequences, which would probably be far more dreadful the second time around. Sam had seen it all before a hundred times while he was going through the care system and growing up as a teenager on the rough streets of Merseyside. On the housing estates, there are lions and there are lambs. The lambs get eaten and that's the end of the story. The only way not to get eaten is not to let the lions see you, and that's where Sam had fucked up. It was too late now. He had drawn their attention, they had seen him, and they had focused their attention on him. As much as he racked his brains trying to look for a way out of this, he really couldn't see an obvious escape.

'I can go back and tell him that you don't think you're responsible for the money that he's lost, if that's what you want me to do, but I'll tell you now, I don't think he'll be very happy with that,' Carla said, shaking her head. 'And I've got to tell you that he is a bit of a nutter at the best of times, but when people owe him money he's just off the scale.'

'Just let me think about this for a minute.' Sam was panicking. He was also fuming inside, angry and helpless. He didn't owe the scumbag any money but if he said he did, how could he say no?

'Think about the alternatives, because they're not good.' Carla shrugged. 'I think you should bite the bullet and take your medicine.' She swung her legs impatiently. 'I'll tell him you don't think you owe the money, and you can take your chances.'

'No. There's no need to tell him that I've said I'm not responsible. I'm trying to think of a better way to put it, or another way of making this straight, without owing any money, if I can.'

'If I was in your shoes, and I'm glad I'm not,' Carla said, shaking her head and smiling. 'I would just pay the money that you owe and put it down to experience.'

'But I don't have any money to spare,' Sam said, shaking his head. 'It's not like I have savings or assets I can liquidate.'

'I know that he's quite open to spreading the cost when people ow him money, but the interest rates are a bit shit, so you would be better off just paying him what you owe him.'

'Did he tell you how much he thinks that I owe him?' Sam asked. He really didn't want to hear the answer, but he would have to ask the question at some point. It was better to know and bite the bullet and then work out what his next step was from there. Whatever the amount was, it was going to be more than he could afford, and he had a funny feeling that the amount would be ridiculously inflated. If you were going to intimidate somebody for money, what's the point of demanding a small amount? You might as well get hung for a sheep as a lamb. He couldn't believe that he was rationalising the fact he was being blackmailed, and trying to make sense of the amount of money that he didn't owe but would have to pay.

'My brother said that Frankie lost about two thousand pounds because the busies were in the street all night and the buyers wouldn't come anywhere near the place. But he said that as a gesture of goodwill, he would call it one thousand five hundred if you pay it all in one go before Sunday.'

'One thousand five hundred pounds before Sunday?' Sam asked, astonished at the amount. He knew it was not going to be good, but he didn't realise exactly how bad it was going to be. He had no idea how much a drug dealer would make in one evening but he didn't think it was that much. How do you tell a drug dealer who is demanding money with menaces that you think he's over exaggerated the amount of money that he's trying to extort from you? It wasn't something that you could take to the Citizens Advice

Bureau or the ombudsman. This was a fight or flight moment. Pay the money and live or don't pay the money and face the consequences. The fact that he looked like the elephant man at the moment was making him lean more towards trying to pay the debt, but he had no way of raising that amount in six months, let alone four days. He had bought his car for £700 the year before and he didn't think it was going to get through the MOT the next time round. It was literally worth the scrap value and nothing more. He didn't own anything else. He had nothing to sell and no other way of raising the cash. Borrowing the money from a legitimate source was out of the question as his credit rating was crap. Nobody would lend him any money at his age on the wages that he earned. That left the option of borrowing the money from a non-legitimate source but that would be even worse than the situation he was in now. The loan sharks on the estate were brutal and took no prisoners and their interest rates ran into the thousand percent. Figures that he could not even understand.

'Shall I tell him that you're not going to pay him then?' Carla asked, tilting her head to one side, like a dog when they look confused.

'I would prefer you not to tell him that as that's not going to help my situation one little bit,' Sam said. 'I've got a few friends that might be able to help me,' Sam said, lying through his teeth. 'Tell him that I'm sorry that he lost so much business, and I will do my very best to get the money together.'

'That is the best decision you have made today,' Carla said, nodding. She stood up and held out her hand for him to shake. 'Shake on it. Shake it, shake it, never ever break it.'

Sam shook her hand and tried to smile but he couldn't muster one. She turned and walked out of the ward as if she was his best friend and nobody noticed her coming or going. His life had been threatened and money extorted and not a single person had seen anything amiss. He felt sick with remorse for the situation he had created himself by trying to be smarter than Frankie the cuckoo. Now he had to find one thousand five hundred pounds before Sunday.

Chapter 19. Andy

The other night, dear, as I lay sleeping, I dreamed I held, you, in my arms, when I awoke, dear, I was mistaken, so I hung my head and I cried...

ANDY TRIED CALLING the number back, but it was disconnected. There was no answerphone and no engaged tone, it was dead. The only explanation was that the owner had taken out the SIM card and snapped it. It must have been a burner phone. Lucy had sounded frightened and confused and the bastard who had her wanted him to feel exactly what she was feeling. Very confused and very frightened. The man had said he was called Jim, but Andy didn't know anyone called Jim. This was all to do with the drug dealer in the ground floor flat. They had sent him packing the night before and Sam had had his face caved in for his troubles. Andy had supported him when he would have been better to stay indoors and let Sam put himself in danger. It had been ridiculous, to put himself in the firing line. He thought Lucy had been safe and sound in the playground at school where she should be, but he couldn't have been further from the truth. He had put her in danger and felt sick with fear. She said the man had picked her up and lifted her over the fence. Had he abducted his daughter because of an altercation with a dealer who had cuckooed their building? How fucked up were these people?

Andy was driving as fast as he dared back towards the school, but the traffic was heavy, and he couldn't make progress. He dialled the school and waited for the reception to answer. It rang and rang but no one answered. He knew the staff were all on the playground in the mornings and the admin staff didn't start until ten as a cost- saving effort. He tried the number again, nothing.

It took him fifteen minutes to reach the school gates and he stopped the van on double-yellow lines. A traffic warden was monitoring the drop off points close to the school, waiting for late arrivals to park illegally and pounce on them. Andy put the handbrake on and jumped out of the door.

'You can't park there, mate,' the warden shouted, waving his hand. 'Can't you see the double-yellow lines?'

'My daughter has been kidnapped,' Andy shouted. The traffic warden looked baffled and a little shocked. He ran towards the gate and Miss Pulmer looked confused. 'A man has taken Lucy from the playground,' Andy said, panicking. 'He called me on my phone, and she said he had lifted her over the fence. Where was she playing?'

'She was with Emma over there at the far side of the playground, under the trees,' Miss Pulmer said, pointing. She got on her radio and called on alert. The school bells rang, and the children were lined up and marched into the building while the staff combed the perimeter of the playground, looking for the two girls. Andy ran along the pavement to the spot near where Miss Pulmer had pointed to. The street was lined with vehicles but there was no one to be seen. He looked over the fence. The grass was covered with dead leaves and sweet wrappers and discarded pizza boxes.

A large van approached, its wheels splashing in the rain, it was travelling much faster than it should have been. Andy watched it skid to a halt in front of a tyre bay across the road. The driver left the engine running and jumped down from the van, running into the tyre shop for whatever reason he had. A Volkswagen Beetle trundled by in the opposite direction, the female driver was blonde and pretty and completely unaware that he had lost his daughter. He had images in his mind of all the abductions he had ever seen on the news; every parent's darkest nightmare was to lose their children and never know what had happened to them. It was a subject that he had always tried to avoid, he never read the news articles about missing children and if they came on the television, he changed the channel because he just couldn't cope with the idea of somebody taking Lucy.

'Lucy!' Andy shouted. He ran along the pavement, ducking low to see inside the parked vehicles. The caller had a twenty-five-minute head start and could be halfway along the M62 by now. He felt like his heart had been ripped out. It was the most desperate, gut-wrenching feeling he had ever experienced. His mouth opened and he looked up and down the road a dozen times, hoping beyond all hope that she was standing somewhere, and he had missed her. Lucy was his life, the reason he got out of bed in the morning, his best friend, his entire being revolved around that child. And she was gone.

Chapter 20. Lenny

When skies are grey, you'll never know, dear, how much I love you…

LENNY SAID GOODBYE to Jo and kissed her on the cheek before leaving the house. She was working at home again today, which she enjoyed as she got more work done than she did in the office. She said that when she was in the office there was always an interruption, people stopping to chat, people stopping to ask a question, people just being people, which slowed down her productivity.

They had enjoyed a few glasses of wine the night before and chatted until just before midnight about Lenny's situation and what was the best way forward. It was a difficult one to deal with. Their first instincts were to stand up to the bullies, the killers, the drug-dealing psychopaths, and help the police to lock them up. In the cold light of day, the fact that these people were violent and lived in a violent world ruled by violent people, meant that standing up against them was a very brave or very stupid thing to do. The easy option was to withdraw his statement and walk away and hope that the gangsters forgot about him in time. The world was changing quickly for the organised crime gangs of Merseyside. There had been a paradigm shift in power and the cyclone of violence continued to blow as the potential kings of the underworld battled it out amongst themselves. It was a dangerous world to be involved in and Lenny wanted no part of it.

Lenny and Jo, were just two normal people trying to live normal lives in the peace and safety of their own home. The looming shadow of violence hanging over their heads made them feel anxious and afraid and nobody should be afraid all day and all night. But the situation wouldn't resolve itself, it would have to be resolved one way or the other and Lenny and Jo could not resolve it by themselves. They would need the help of the police if they were to stay safe and lift the threat that hung over them.

Lenny drove to the matrix unit at Speke for the second day running. He was nervous as he knew that the previous day, he had been followed by the two gorillas that had confronted him at the car auction. Every car that he saw in his rear view mirror was a threat and he checked each driver to see if he could recognise them. The men that had followed him the previous day were using a vehicle with false plates and the police had not been able to trace them. It was a worry to say the least and he had discussed the situation with Detective Inspector Chrissie Dunn, and they had agreed that it might be best if he went back to the identification suite to see if he could recognise any of the mug shots, and match them up to the men that he had encountered the day before.

He went to the reception and announced himself, and Chrissie was approaching him within a few minutes. He had hardly had time to sit down. She smiled when she approached but her face showed the concern that she felt for the situation that they were in.

'First of all, let me tell you how sorry I am that we are in this situation,' Chrissy said. 'I didn't anticipate them following you before you had even had the chance to identify the men that attacked you, which tells me that they were worried that you would come to us anyway.'

'There's no need for you to apologise on behalf of a bunch of thugs. Thugs do what thugs do and they think they can get away with it because nine times out of ten, they do get away with it.'

'I don't think it's as high as nine,' Chrissie frowned.

'Eight?'

'I'm sticking at seven.'

'Okay, we'll agree to disagree.' Lenny nodded. 'You're not a fortune teller and you can't predict the future, so we'll just have to take it on the chin and come up with a Plan B.' Lenny stood up and put his hands in his pockets. He smiled but his eyes looked tired, and they were tinged with concern. 'I had a good chat with Jo last night, and no matter how many times we talk around it, we both think that walking away from this now is probably more dangerous can staying on the course.'

'It's a relief you feel that way. I would understand if you had doubts.'

'We have plenty of doubts.'

'We will protect you to the best of our ability. You have my word on that.'

'I trust you at your word.'

'Shall we go through and see Yasmin again? We'll see if we can't find the two idiots who threatened you yesterday.'

They walked through the reception area just as they had the previous day, and then navigated the maze of corridors to the identification suite. Chrissie opened the door and stepped back to let Lenny in. Yasmin waved hello.

'Hello, back so soon,' she said.

'Hello Yasmin. I wasn't expecting to be back so soon, but here I am. I'm hoping that somewhere in your selection of mug shots, you will have an image of the gorillas I encountered yesterday.'

'It's nice to see you, no matter what the circumstances. I'm going to try my best to narrow it down and find an image that you recognise.'

'That sounds good to me.'

'I have narrowed it down to less than thirty images. They're all men known to have worked for Barry Maddern and his associates. It's not going to take us long, and they will either be in there or they won't.'

'I have a feeling they will be in there.'

'What makes you so sure?' Chrissie asked.

'Because they're stupid,' Lenny said.

'There's no point going on a fishing expedition in this situation. It's easier to narrow down the field and focus on possible culprits.'

'It makes sense to me,' Lenny said, sitting down on the same chair that he had used the day before. 'This seat is still warm from yesterday,' Lenny said, joking. He picked up a bottle of water from the table and twisted the top off. Taking a sip, he gestured towards the screen. 'Let's go. I'm ready when you are, Yasmin.'

The format was the same as the previous day, two rows of three mug shots appeared on the screen at the same time. The doubts and indecision sprang into his mind immediately. That face looked familiar, another looked like somebody he knew but wasn't actually them, and another face reminded him of somebody that he had seen in a film or maybe in a band. His brain was playing tricks on him. He shook his head to let Yasmin know that he didn't recognise any of the first six.

The second six appeared and Lenny laughed out loud, pointing to the top right of the screen.

'Bingo.'

'You recognise him?'

'I told you that there were two of them and one of them was wearing a pair of mirrored Ray-Ban sunglasses, trying to disguise himself. The other guy didn't try as hard,' Lenny said smiling. 'That is the guy who didn't try to disguise himself. He was a real whopper. That is him.'

'Sure?'

'Yes. He has those stary eyes with a slight turn in the left. I'm absolutely certain that's him.'

'That is excellent Lenny. He is Daniel Nathan, and he is just out after a fifteen-year stretch for a string of armed robberies on security vans.'

'Sounds like a real diamond.'

'The good news is, he only works with his brother Theo. Have we got an image of him?'

Yasmin tapped at her laptop for a few seconds, deleted five of the images and added one more. The two men looked alike, and it was obvious that they were related.

'That is Sunglasses,' Lenny said pointing to the second man. 'Even with the hat and sunglasses on I can identify him. He is the man who said I was a dead man walking.'

'One hundred percent?'

'One thousand. Please tell me you know where they live.'

'Absolutely, we know where they live. I guarantee that before you get home today,' Chrissie said, nodding, 'they will be in the cells. And I'll make damn sure that they don't make bail.'

Chapter 21. Heather Norris

Don't leave me this way, no I can't exist ...

HEATHER HAD LOST TRACK of time, looking at Hope through the window in the critical-care unit. It had broken her heart to see her little girl lying there with tubes going into places they shouldn't be. Phil had let her stay there as long as she wanted to, which she hadn't expected as he was usually a prick. She didn't like him, and she never would, and she only tolerated him because he had the power to remove her children from her. He thought she was a bad mum. She could see it in his eyes when she looked at him, but what he didn't realise was that Heather was struggling with life. There was probably some fancy diagnosis for the way that her mind worked. She didn't function as she should, and she knew it was all in their mind. She wasn't physically ill. She didn't suffer any pain, but there were some mornings when she didn't want to wake up, let alone get out of bed and be a parent. There were days when she wished she was dead. Facing the challenge of a full day dealing with other human beings was overwhelming for her. She wanted to close her eyes, pull the quilt over her body, and stay in bed. The responsibility of being a parent was too much for her and that twisted her up inside. She loved her children, and she knew that they loved her unconditionally, but she saw how disappointed they were when there was no milk in the fridge and no electricity in the meter. Seeing disappointment in the eyes of your children is the most soul-destroying experience she had felt as a parent. She wished there was a way that she could explain how she felt to Phil and to his boss Jo Lilly, but she could never find the words. When they were talking to her about her lack of response to the actions that they said needed to be put into place, her brain would switch off. They had recorded many times that she wasn't engaging in the child protection plan, which was aimed at making sure her family stayed together, but they just didn't understand. She wasn't engaging because she couldn't function. Being dragged to the police station was the last thing she wanted. They were going to ask her the same questions over and over, but the answers would be the same.

Heather was sitting in the same seat that David had been sat in earlier and she had the same brief, Howell Jones. It had been deemed that using the same solicitor to represent both adults made sense as he already had an understanding of the incident that happened at the Norris home on the morning that Hope had been shot. Heather was waiting to be interviewed and she felt very anxious. She felt as if she was being interrogated unfairly. The police and social services were picking on her and trying to make her look guilty. She was worried that she would say something stupid, which would make them believe that she was.

DI Jane Bennett came into the room with another detective who Heather had never seen before. The detectives were friendly enough on the surface but she felt their eyes probing hers. She knew what they were thinking. They were thinking she was a bad mother and that she drank too much alcohol and smoked weed, and both of those things broke the conditions of the child protection plan. Phil Moult had sent her for a hair strand test the week before to see if she was taking anything else. She had told him not to waste his time and money because she had been smoking weed but nothing else. David was another story. She had her suspicions that he was taking something. He had been spending a lot of time at the bookmakers lately, which she didn't like. He had been winning and had money for alcohol and cannabis, so she kept her mouth shut. They wouldn't be able to afford it otherwise. Cannabis was the only thing that calmed her down enough to function. Smoking a bit of weed was hardly the crime of the century and she doubted very much if they would take her children away from her because she had smoked a spliff.

'I'm DI Jane Bennett for the sake of the recording. We are speaking to Heather Norris in relation to an assault at her home.'

'It was outside my home on the street,' Heather said. 'Let's get that straight. It was on the road, and I was in the house, in bed.'

'Your daughter, Hope Norris, was hit in the face by a lead projectile, fired from a close distance by an air rifle.' Jane paused and looked up. 'Before we start, Heather, I want to say how sorry I am that your daughter is in the critical-care unit. I'm glad that you had the opportunity to see her before you came here. I want to clear up a few things as quickly as possible because your social worker, Phil, is very keen that you are back at home before your other three children get home from school.'

'He's such a hero,' Heather said, sarcastically. 'I practically had to beg the twat to let me see my daughter in intensive care. That's not right, but let's get it on tape, shall we?'

'Yes quite,' Jane mumbled. 'So, let's do this as quickly as we can, with as little fuss as possible.'

'That's fine by me. I don't want to be here at all, and I don't even know why I am,' Heather said, shaking her head. 'David has told you that he didn't take the air rifle from the wardrobe, which means he didn't shoot Hope. So, why am I here?'

'We have to check every possibility when an incident of this gravity has occurred, and I'm sure if you think about it, you can understand what we are doing is making sure that another child does not get shot.'

'I realise that you have got a job to do, but you should be looking elsewhere to find who shot my daughter.'

'Elsewhere?' Jane asked.

'The people in the two houses behind ours both have air rifles, and they shoot at cans against the fence all the time.'

'We'll be speaking to all the neighbours in due course.'

'You should do. A neighbour's cat was found dead the other month, and they were convinced it had been hit in the head with a pellet but there was no pellet.'

'I don't understand.'

'The pellet might have ricocheted off, so they couldn't prove it, but the vet said the cat had been hit in the head with something small and powerful.' Heather looked at her solicitor as if she was expecting him to say something. 'If that isn't enough evidence for you to be looking elsewhere, then I don't know what is.'

'As I said, we'll be speaking to your neighbours.'

'You should be speaking to them, not me,' Heather said. 'Aren't you supposed to be defending me?' she asked Howell. He shook his head.

'I'm here to represent you and give you the best advice that I can give and my advice to you at this moment in time, is to answer DI Bennett as truthfully as you can, so that she can get to the bottom of who fired an air rifle towards the road when your daughter was shot. I think that is what everybody in this room is hoping for.'

'Absolutely that is what we are hoping for,' Jane said. 'We're not on a witch hunt. Let's get to the crux of the matter, and we can get this wrapped up as quickly as possible.'

'Hurry up then,' Heather said, folding her arms.

'You were in bed when the children got dressed, had breakfast and then left for school?'

'Yes,' Heather said nodding. She blushed, embarrassed. 'I wasn't feeling well.'

'Did you hear anything that was said in the kitchen between David and your children?'

'No, I was asleep.'

'Did you hear the children leaving the house to walk to school?'

'No. I've just told you that I was asleep, and I didn't hear a thing. I struggle in the morning, and I have difficulty waking up without feeling like my head is full of cotton wool. I can't focus on anything for an hour or so.'

'So, what is the first thing that you can remember about that morning?' Jane asked.

'I'm not sure what order things happened in, but I remember David coming into the room telling me to get out of bed because something had happened to Hope.'

'You don't remember David coming into the room with a glass of water, saying that you had the house to yourselves and there were no kids?' Heather frowned. 'He said you were fooling around in bed?'

'No, I don't remember that.' Heather blushed and looked down at the table. 'That stuff is private. None of your business.'

'It's important to the sequence of events.' Heather twiddled her fingers. 'David said that you were fooling around under the covers, when the kids came back into the house to tell you what had happened to Hope?'

'If he says that's what happened, then that's what happened,' Heather said, nodding. 'I told you that I struggle to get going in the morning. I get a fog of sleep, which doesn't lift for a long time. My memory is probably blurry because I had only just woken up.'

'Just to clarify, the first thing that you can remember is being told that something had happened to Hope outside on the street?'

'Yes.'

'David didn't come into the bedroom with a glass of water. He didn't go to the wardrobe and take out the air rifle at any point?'

'I've just told you. David came into the room and told me that something had happened to Hope and that I had to get out of bed. That is how I remember it. If he says he came in with a glass of water and got back into bed for a cuddle, then that is what happened, but at no point did he go near the air rifle.'

'But you said it was foggy and you're not sure,' Jane said. 'But now, you're sure?'

'Do you think I would be sitting here defending him if he had shot my daughter in the face with that gun?' Heather waited for a response, but the detectives just looked at her waiting for her to speak. Allowing a witness to try and fill the silence in the room can pay dividends in an investigation. They were waiting for Heather to say something which contradicted what David had said or what she had said herself. 'I might not be mother of the year, and I don't pretend to be and I'm not saying that David is the best stepdad either, but he didn't shoot my daughter. I am not trying to defend him.' There was an uncomfortable silence. 'Now can I go home and make tea for my children please?'

Chapter 22. The Devil

The devil went down to Georgia, he was looking for a soul to steal, he was in a bind because he was way behind, and he was willing to make a deal...

FRANKIE WILLS WAS WITH Andrew Head in a cafe down the road from the block of flats where Sam and Mary lived. They had been watching uniformed police officers knocking on doors in the street, asking questions about gang activity and the abduction and murder of Anthony Head. Andrew was sick to the back teeth of listening to his mother waffling on the phone to family members, about what had happened to his father. The truth was nobody knew what had happened to him, but every member of the family seems to have a different opinion on his murder. It was good for his mother to talk about what had happened to his father, her husband of 25 years. She had been in bits from the day that they realised he wasn't coming home. He had left the house to go for a pint with a mate, or so he said, but the police had never been able to find the mate he was supposed to be meeting. Andrew was a bright kid, and he knew that there was more to his disappearance than met the eye, but when he broached the subject with his mum, she would get angry and shout, and say that he was being disrespectful to his father. He wasn't being disrespectful but something untoward happened to him for a reason.

When the police had come to the house to tell them that they had identified his body, she was stunned. They had used a photograph that the family had given to them. His mother was distraught that they hadn't asked her to identify her husband. She gave the detectives a really hard time and they did their best to soften the blow, but she just wouldn't let the subject go. Eventually, they had to tell her that her husband had been decapitated and dismembered. They had made the decision not to ask a family member to identify him until, they were sure. Of course, his mother had insisted on going to identify him herself and it had broken her.

Andrew couldn't stay in the house for more than a few hours as it was just too traumatic. She was in hysterics most of the time. Listening to his mother suffering so much pain and loss was horrendous. He had decided to spend as much time out of the house as possible, and he was keeping himself busy. He was doing a bit of work for Frankie Wills, helping deliver bits and pieces here and there. Frankie and his friends ran a big business, which was selling ketamine and cocaine. Andrew knew what they did for a living, and he was okay with it. Everybody was taking ketamine or coke and some people were making big money from supplying it. Frankie Wills was one of those people. Frankie was a top guy. He was funny and hard as nails and always had designer gear and nice cars. He paid Andrew well to make a few short trips a week on his bike and Andrew couldn't see what harm he was doing. The people who were buying their drugs from Frankie would buy them from somewhere. The estate was full of it, so it was better to be a part of it and make some cash, rather than watch someone else making it.

There had been an incident at the flats a few nights before and some of the residents had told Frankie they were going to talk to the police. Sam said that when the police came knocking, he was going to tell them when Frankie had arrived in the building, what he was doing, and give them the names of the teenagers who were visiting him. He had never seen Frankie so angry as he was that night, and he was raging and ranting. Frankie had stashed some gear in his car, which was parked by the shops, and then gone back to the building to confront the residents. Sam, the guy who lived upstairs, had been standing in the front window, and Frankie said he could not miss the opportunity to shut him up once and for all. He had thrown a brick through the window. The brick hit him square in the face and it had caused a real kerfuffle, with the police and an ambulance being called. There were blue lights flashing on the street for hours, which kept the customers away. Frankie had told them that that wasn't the end of the matter. He said there were three residents who had said they were going to grass him up. He wanted them all dealt with and silenced. There were too many police canvassing the area to mess about and take a chance that one of them started talking. They needed to be silenced.

Frankie already had a date with Crown Court coming up and three outstanding warrants with his name on them. He couldn't risk being investigated for distribution or possession with intent to supply. If he was nicked on either of those two offences, he would not get bail and would be locked up, looking at a long sentence. He had no intentions of going to jail.

Carla walked into the cafe and made a beeline for the table they were sitting at. Andrew wouldn't admit it to the other lads, but he had a crush on her. He didn't want to say anything because her brother was a nutcase and had battered a guy who had asked her out a few months before. Apparently, he had been in the Paras. Carla looked pleased with herself as she sat down. The waitress came over and Carla ordered a latte.

'Did you get the pictures that I sent you from the hospital?' she asked, smiling. Frankie nodded and squeezed her arse. 'Get off.'

'You love it.'

'You wish.'

'How did it go?'

'I found out the ward Sam was on, and I waited until visiting time to go and see him. It was a doddle getting in there. He was sitting on his bed looking sorry for himself. His face is a right mess, and they reckon he has fractured his skull at the back and broken his nose.'

'It was a good shot,' Frankie laughed.

'It was a lucky shot,' Carla joked. 'Both his eyes are black and nearly closed, man. You should see them. He looks like he's been in the ring with Tyson.' She paused. 'Did you show Andrew the pictures, or what?'

'Not yet. Take a look at them,' Frankie said, handing Andrew his phone. He swiped through the images, laughing. 'That is what happens to a fool threatening to go to the police.'

'That is sick, man,' Andrew said as he looked through the images of Sam's battered face. 'That man is not gonna say a word about anything, I'm telling you that now. Just look at the state of his nose! Wicked, man.'

Andrew laughed a bit too long and a bit too hard, but he was trying to impress Carla. She was watching him at the same time as he was watching her, but she knew Frankie had his eyes on him. Frankie had a thing for teenage boys, and he had told her he was going to fuck Andrew. The attraction was clear to anyone watching, except Andrew. He wasn't the first courier to attract Frankie's attention and straight or not, they all succumbed, willing or not.

'So, Frankie, tell me where we're going to set up now we've lost the flat?' Carla asked. 'I've been getting text messages all morning from people asking where we're going to be selling from tonight.' Her latte arrived, and she sipped it. She frowned at the flavour and added three spoonfuls of sugar to the cup.

'You don't need to worry about where we're going to set up because it's all in hand, isn't it Andrew?' Andrew nodded and smiled, blushing a little bit. 'You see, Andrew here sent a little message from me to the old bird who lives in the downstairs flat. She took a little tumble.'

'No way,' Carla said.

'A little dickie bird at the hospital told me that she has a broken hip. At her age, a broken hip is a serious issue and she's probably going to be in the hospital for six weeks or so.'

'No way have you put two of the people from the flats in the hospital,' Carla said laughing. 'That is quality. You're a beast.'

'You are a beast,' Andrew agreed. 'You're the main man.' Carla could see how Andrew looked up to Frankie. He had been groomed but he had no idea what was coming. She felt sorry for him. It was going to come as a surprise to him. Frankie would manufacture an opportunity to be alone with Andrew and then he would pounce. He had cornered Carla several times and when she resisted, he turned violent. She was forced to suck his cock the first time, but his attention soon moved on to someone else. He had never tried to fuck her, which was a blessing. If he became focused on her nowadays, she offered to masturbate him. Once he had finished, the relationship went back to normal as if nothing had happened. She didn't think Andrew was going to get away so lightly.

'So, the old lady has bust her hip and is going to be laid up for a while?'

'Thanks to Andrew' Frankie said, smiling at him. 'I've got a special bonus in mind for you.'

'Really?' Andrew asked, blushing.

'I don't see that what that has to do with where we're gonna set up?' Carla tried to drag the conversation back to the real world. 'What are you planning?'

'When the old lady fell over, she dropped her bag, and Andrew, being the kind considerate lad that he is, picked it up.'

'This kid is sharp,' Carla said.

'He is my new number one,' Frankie said.

Poor fucker, Carla thought.

'So, we have an empty flat, which is furnished and heated and has hot water and a nice clean toilet. It will have milk in the fridge and tea in the cupboard and we'll be nice and cosy in there for a while.'

'Oh my God, that is so cool,' Carla said clapping her hands. 'We were sleeping on the floor in the last place, and it was freezing.'

'That's not all, because in her purse is her debit card and it's contactless. So, coffee and breakfast is on me,' Frankie said, looking at the debit card. 'To be honest it's not actually on me, it's on Mary Dennis. So, thank you very much, Mary.' He handed the debit card to Carla. 'I want you to keep hold of this. Get us a couple of litres of vodka, not the shit stuff, and eighty cigarettes, and bring them to the flat in a couple of hours.'

'Okay. What are you doing?' Carla asked.

'Me and Andrew are going to go there now and make ourselves at home for a while, aren't we mate?'

'Whatever you say,' Andrew said, nodding. 'You're the boss.'

'I am,' Frankie said, nodding. He winked at Carla, and she felt sick. 'No rush for you to get there. We'll wait for you there and start bagging up a few kilos. Keep your purchases under a hundred pounds and that card will keep working.'

'Okay,' Carla said, standing up. She wanted to tell Andrew he was about to take a walk on the wild side, but she liked her teeth where they were.

'We've also got a card for a savings account, so we're gonna need the pin number from Mary for that. Give her a few days to settle in the hospital and then go and have a little word with her. It shouldn't be too hard to convince her to give us the pin number, or the same thing could happen to her again when she gets out, and no one wants that.'

'Andrew might enjoy doing that for you, seeing as he's your new number one,' Carla said, walking away. 'Have fun, guys. Don't do anything I wouldn't do.'

Chapter 23. Kidnap

Hello darkness, my old friend, I've come to talk with you again...

RUPERT STOKES HAD NEVER been so scared in his life. He was blindfolded and sitting in the back of a van with his hands zip-tied behind his back. His nose was bleeding, and he was finding it difficult to breathe. Earlier that day he had been sitting in his living room minding his own business, when he had heard the knock on the back door. It was unusual for anybody to go around the back of the house, and so he thought that it was some of the local kids up to mischief again. There had been a spate of shed break-ins in the area and random acts of vandalism to greenhouses, outhouses and garden ornaments. Dozens of garden gnomes had gone missing, and the residents were putting it down to mischievous kids from the neighbouring council estate. Rupert didn't have any children and he had no intentions of having any. He didn't know an awful lot about parenting but what he did know was, that the kids from the local council state were no worse behaved then the kids who belonged to his neighbours. They were ignorant and arrogant, and he wouldn't trust them with his wheelie bin.

When he opened the back door, he was expecting to see a teenager. Obviously, it wasn't a teenager at the back door, it was a huge black man. He punched him in the nose before he could even speak. The blow had stunned him and knocked him backwards and he had ended up sitting on the floor in his kitchen. He had been tied up and a bag put over his head before he knew what day it was.

There were three men. He could tell from their voices. Listening to what they were saying gave him the impression that they were very organised. One of them had said that they would take his car, so that the police would think he had left his house of his own accord. That didn't sound like a good thing to Rupert. It sounded like something that he would hear in one of the gangster movies that he loved so much on Netflix. It was one thing getting armchair thrills, but it was completely different to being involved in a criminal abduction, especially when he was the abductee.

Rupert was a clever man, and he was under no illusions as to who had taken him from his home. The police had been to his place of work following an anonymous tip off and searched one of the units on the first floor. What they had found in there was obviously the reason why he had been kidnapped and bundled into the back of a van. The police said they had found a body in a fridge freezer, and they also said that something had been removed from the unit recently.

Rupert had taken a cash payment from the men who had hired the unit initially. They had paid him to make sure that no visits to the unit were ever recorded either on film or in the computer database, and he had stuck to his side of the bargain. He could only hope that the men who had abducted him would realise that he was no threat to their security and that their secret was safe with him.

It felt as if they had been driving for hours and some of it had definitely been on the motorway, which was concerning as the further away from home they went, the more frightened he was becoming. There were only a couple of reasons why anybody would go to the trouble of organising the abduction of an average Joe from his home. None of them were pleasant. He had asked the man why they were taking him and received another punch in the face for his trouble, so deemed it was better to keep quiet. Everything would come clear eventually, he thought.

He felt the van climbing a gradient and it became difficult to sit upright. The vehicle slowed as the gradient became steeper and he could hear the driver dropping through the gears to keep the van moving up the slope. The sound of tree branches banging and scraping against the roof of the van became louder and louder. It was clear that they had driven to a woodland area, which didn't bode well. Being an abductee and realising that you had been driven to a forest sent shockwaves running through his mind, that there might not be a way out of this situation. This could be the last few minutes of his life. Nobody would know how he died or where his body was buried, and that made him feel sad. He was an only child and although he didn't have a great relationship with his dad, his mother was his world. When he had come out to his parents as being gay his mother had said that she'd known all along, probably since he was five or six. His father had been a different kettle of fish, and his actual words were that he had never been so disappointed in anything in all his life. That had been difficult to deal with for both of them, and their relationship as father and son had never been the same since. Unfortunately, it also meant that he hadn't seen his mum as often as he should or wanted to. Whatever their differences, he was sure that his father would want to know where he was buried and why he had been killed. The thought of them not knowing made him feel desperately sad.

Rupert felt the van slow to a halt, and then he heard the engine being turned off. One of the men said that he had been there before, and the ground was softer about 200 yards up the path to the left. Another one said there was already a hole dug. That sent fear streaking through Rupert, and he felt like he was going to have a heart attack. He had never experienced anything like it. His mortality was staring him in the face in the darkness of his hood. This was it. This was the end of an unremarkable life, which was coming to a remarkable end that no one would witness. He wondered how it was going to end, if they would shoot him, or stab him, or choke him to death, or hit him over the head with something heavy. Whatever death they had in mind for him, he just hoped and prayed that it would be quick. He didn't like pain and the thought of being buried alive made him feel like he was going to puke right there in the back of the van.

Rupert heard the back door open and strong hands grabbed his arms and pulled him towards the back door. He was bundled out of the van and fell to his knees. They pulled him up to his feet without saying a word and led him away from the van, his feet hardly touching the ground. From beneath the hood, he could see his own feet walking one foot in front of the other. The ground was dark and peaty, crisscrossed with fallen twigs and rotting leaves. The distinctive smell of pine needles reached him, and he guessed that they had driven him to Delamere Forest up in the hills above Frodsham. It was one of his favourite places to visit as a child; his parents would make a picnic and they would sit on one of the wooden benches, eat their food, drink hot tea from a flask and watch the red squirrels looking for acorns beneath the trees. But that was a long time ago when he was a child, and the world didn't seem so violent. He never thought for one minute that the end of his life would be manufactured by the hands of another human being. That wasn't the world that he had been brought up in, or the world that he had spent his time as an adult in. It all changed when he had taken that cash.

He knew at the time he was making a big mistake, but he hadn't had a pay rise from his employers for years, he had missed his bonus targets, and greed made the choice for him that day.

He was made to walk for about 10 minutes along the path and then he was led through the trees to a clearing, where the forest wasn't so dense. He could hardly breathe as he waited for what was going to happen next. His senses were ultra-aware as he waited for a bullet to smash through his brain, or to feel cold steel piercing his flesh as a knife ripped his abdomen open but neither of those things happened.

'Take the hood off him,' one of the men said. The hood was removed, and Rupert had to blink his eyes against the glare of the daylight. It was a grey day, and a light drizzle was falling but daylight and rain had never felt so good. He was absolutely convinced that the last moments of his life were going to be spent in the darkness of that hood. Feeling the raindrops on his face felt like it had never felt before. He looked around at the faces of the three men who had brought him into this place and no attempt to hide their identity had been made.

'OK Rupert, this is a grave which we dug a few weeks back,' the black man said, pointing to an oblong hole a few yards away. 'It should have been occupied by now, but circumstances changed and here you are. Sit down on the edge of the hole,' the man said, pointing.

Rupert was led to the edge of the grave, and they forced him to sit down with his feet in the hole. It was the most bizarre feeling that he had ever had, staring into the dank soil where he was going to lie for eternity. How many people get to see their own grave?

His brain was screaming at him to struggle, to resist, to try and run as fast as he could in a final attempt to stay on this planet for a little bit longer, but his muscles were frozen with fear. It was ridiculous when people said, I would do this, and I would do that, and I would do the other, but the harsh reality is, that in times of mortal fear, most people freeze and are compliant.

'Why are you doing this to me?' Rupert asked, finally finding his voice. 'What did I do wrong?'

'We're here to ask you some questions and depending on what your answers are, we have to decide whether you're going back home in the van or if we're going to bury you in that hole.'

'Obviously, I want to go home, so ask me whatever questions you need to, and I will answer them. I don't want to die.'

'In which case you need to get the answers right, Rupert. Our boss is looking for some people who are trying to stitch him up. Let's start at the beginning.'

'Okay.'

'The police came into your facility, and they searched a storage unit.'

'Yes.'

'How did they know which unit they were going to search?'

'They had a warrant to search that specific unit, so they must have known which unit to go to before they arrived.'

'How do you think they knew?'

'One of the detectives told me that they had had an anonymous tip off.'

'Who was in charge of the search?'

'Detective Chief Inspector French, and there were two other detectives with him, one was called Evans and there was a woman called Talbot.'

'When that unit was rented, you were given an amount of cash in twenty-pound notes and an arrangement was made, that there would be no records of anybody visiting that unit. Is that correct?'

'Yes. That's exactly what happened.'

'Have the police examined your financial records and bank accounts yet?'

'They want to investigate all our employees. I think they have done mine because they made an appointment to come to my house to speak to me today, but I haven't spoken to them about my finances yet.'

'When you were given the cash, what did you do with the money?'

'I kept it in a drawer in my bedroom and used it to do my shopping and go to the pub and stuff. I never put any of it into my bank. The guy who gave me the cash insisted that none of it could ever go anywhere near an account, and I stuck to that, honestly, I did.'

'If you have agreed to speak to the police today about your financial situation, you must realise that they have looked in detail at your finances around the periods that that unit was rented.'

'Yes. I know that, and they won't see any large amounts being paid into it, but there may be a period where I haven't withdrawn as much money from my account as I normally would in a month.'

'That is when you were using the cash?'

'Yes. I suppose they will be able to see that I was funding my life somehow and not using my bank account. And I understand that will look odd.'

'And what have you planned to say to them that will explain how you funded your day-to-day life without using your bank account?'

'I did some research online and I found a horse which ran at Chepstow the same month as I was given the cash. The horse was called Superpower and it won at twenty to one. My plan was to tell them that I had a bet on that horse with the bookies in Prescot. I went to school there so I'm familiar with the area. I know that they will go and try to verify that bet but the bookie traded in a row of shops, which were demolished about twelve months ago. The shop was run by a guy called Corbett, and he died a month after the shop closed. They can't disprove my story.'

The men looked at each other, suitably impressed by the story that Rupert had come up with to explain how he had not used his bank account for a few months.

'That's not a bad story at all, kid,' the man who had asked the question said. 'I think that you could probably get away with that and even if the police persisted, there is enough doubt for it to stand up in court.'

'That is what I think.'

'Which leads me to my next question. Somebody removed something from that unit. We need to know if you saw who it was?'

'Yes, I saw who it was, and it definitely wasn't the same guy who initially rented the unit. He wasn't the guy who gave me the cash either. He came in a van with a driver, who was a big black guy in his fifties, and I hadn't seen him before either.'

'Okay Rupert. I need you to describe the man who went into the unit.'

'He was a big guy, built like a bodybuilder. His arms and hands were all tattooed, and he has a big red star inked beneath his left ear. He had dark brown hair which was shaved at the sides and longer on top, probably over six feet tall and he had Turkey teeth.' The man laughed. 'Do you recognise him?'

'Yes.' There was a pause. 'What did he take from the unit?' the man asked.

'He took a silver travelling trunk. The type with metal protectors on all the corners, and brass clasp locks. You don't see many of them around nowadays, but people used to use them to go travelling and school pupils used them to go to boarding schools.'

'Did anybody else go into that unit that day?'

'No. I have never seen anybody go into that unit from the first day that it was rented. But the day that guy took the trunk, I had a staff member working on reception, so it was easy for me to make sure that the visit wasn't recorded. But if anybody needed to verify my description of the man, then there is another witness.'

'You are doing very well here, Rupert,' the man said, stroking the bristles on his chin. He looked to be thinking about his next step. Rupert had been as open and honest as he could be. There was a glimmer of hope in his heart, that maybe he could survive this experience.

'The police are going to ask you if you saw the man, who rented that unit in person. They are also going to ask you, who physically gave you the money for the rent and if you saw them in person. And they're going to ask you to describe the man who took the trunk from the unit.'

'I've told the police that nobody removed anything from that unit,' Rupert said, shaking his head.

'You're going to change your story, Rupert,' the man said. 'The man that you described taking the trunk is called Gary Booth. It's obvious to me that Gary Booth is the man who gave the police the anonymous tip off about the body in the freezer.'

'I understand.'

'That makes Gary Booth a grass. And if there's one thing that we cannot tolerate in our business, it's a grass. So, we're going to need you to tell the police that Gary Booth removed the trunk and that there is a witness who can verify your story.'

'Okay. I can do that.'

'We're also going to need you to say that the same man paid for the initial rent in person, and he is the only man who has had access to that unit.'

Rupert listened to what the man had to say and mulled it over in his mind. They were asking him to lie to the police and in the process point the finger at this Gary Booth character for the murder of the man in the freezer. He didn't know who this man was, and he didn't care. They were all criminals, and he didn't care whose side they were on, he just needed to make sure that he was going to be in the back of that van and not in the hole that he was sitting in.

'I can do as you ask with absolutely no problems at all. If you take me home, I will call the police and rearrange the interview and I'll explain everything you have just said, and if they ask me why I didn't say it in the first place, I'll just say that I was scared of Gary Booth.'

'Very good, Rupert. I like you. You're a good sort of bloke,' the man said. 'Let's get this kid home safe and sound where he belongs.'

Chapter 24. Andy

In restless dreams I walked alone, narrow streets of cobblestone...

ANDY WAS BESIDE HIMSELF. It had been a full forty minutes since he had arrived at the school. The police had arrived on the scene and a search party was being organised. The school was in a built-up area which was dotted with small patches of woodland, three parks, a deep brook on the railway line which ran into Liverpool city centre. And they could see the expression on the faces of the police detectives, and they were not convinced that the two girls were still in the vicinity of the school. Not for one minute. It was so obvious, but he couldn't understand why they were going through the motions of setting up search parties for people to walk around the circumference of the school grounds for the 20th time that day. The girls were not at the school. They were not hiding. They were not playing games. They were simply gone. The only way a strange man could get two intelligent children away from the school without attracting any attention to himself, was in a vehicle.

Andy was on the verge of having a meltdown. He wanted to get in his van and drive. It just seemed pointless staying so close to the school when it was obvious that the girls were no longer in the area. The lead detective had asked him the same questions over and over again. What did the man say, what did he sound like, what was his name, did you recognise him, do you know anybody called Jim?

If he asked him one of those questions again, he would scream. Andy watched as one group set off following the school fence to the left while a second group followed the school fence to the right. The groups were a mixture of uniformed police officers, teachers and parents. Everybody was playing the incident down and telling Andy not to worry because the girls couldn't have got far. It was the most ridiculous thing that you could say to the parent of a missing child. Don't worry.

Fuck off.

A detective was talking on his phone about fifty yards away from Andy; the expression on his face changed to one of concern. It was obvious that the call was bringing bad news. Andy walked towards him, and the detective saw him coming and gestured him over. A group of uniformed officers were making their way across the playground on the other side of the fence. One of them was carrying something in his hand. The detective finished his call and walked towards Andy.

'They have found a shoe stuck in the railings of the fence over there beneath the trees where the teacher said she last saw the two girls playing.'

Andy's heart sank and he felt physically sick as the uniformed officers approached. He was staring at the shoe the officer was holding in his right hand. Something pink was hanging from the shoe.

'What type of shoes was your daughter wearing this morning?' the Detective asked, frowning.

'She was wearing a pair of cherry red boots.' Andy could hardly hear anything that anybody was saying. His hearing had gone completely fuzzy and all he could focus on was the red boot in the policeman's hand and the pink sock that was hanging from it. He knew the sock belonged to Lucy because it wasn't one of her favourites and it was the reason she had kicked off when she was getting ready for school that morning. He would give anything to hear her kicking off again. Anything at all.

Chapter 25. Lenny

And in the naked light I saw, ten thousand people, maybe more...

LENNY WAS BACK AT THE auction, and he was convinced that nobody had followed him this time. He had left the matrix unit, feeling convinced that the police had everything in hand. Theo and Daniel Nathan were a couple of hardened criminals brought up on the back streets of Anfield. They had been petty criminals for most of their lives, dabbled in amateur boxing and football, but they weren't good enough to make it as professionals in either sport. In their early twenties, they had attached themselves to an up-and-coming organised crime gang, working out of the Anfield and Kensington areas. Neither of the brothers had the capacity to be leaders and they were used as battering rams and enforcers for most of their criminal careers. Until they realised that people who had joined the organisation after them were being promoted above them, and were earning a lot more money than they were. It was at that point that they decided they would go it alone and for the next ten years, they organised and carried out a string of armed robberies, mostly on soft targets. They found that robbing McDonald's drive-thrus was easy money until the arrival of debit cards. As cash started going into decline, so did the opportunity to commit armed robberies. The only feasible targets left to rob were the armoured vehicles, which carried all the cash. The problem with armoured vehicles was, they were no longer easy to rob and the chances of being caught in possession of smart money were high. It was simply a matter of time and the brothers got caught and were sentenced to fifteen years. They hadn't been out long when Maddern was arrested.

When Barry Maddern and his lieutenants were arrested, the Nathan brothers were left on the streets, as it was deemed by the police that they had not long come out of prison and were not deep enough into the organisation to warrant them being arrested. They had been sitting on the sidelines, being fed crumbs from the table where they had once sat. It appeared that they had been ordered to follow Lenny and put the pressure on, probably because they were two of only a handful of the outfit who were still on the streets. They certainly weren't sent because they were the best at the job.

Lenny parked up the Jag, making sure that it was underneath one of the many cameras, and he made his way towards the burger van. As he approached, Della saw him coming and she waved at him with a big smile on her face. It was nice to know that people were genuinely pleased to see him back in the saddle. Lenny decided to wait before going to the burger van as he wanted to take a good look at some of the Porsches which were in the auction catalogue before the other dealers arrived. Porsches were always in demand no matter how old they were or which model. They could be bought cheaply enough to make a decent profit on them when they were sold on. He made his way around the back of the sale room to where the four acres of car parks were. There were cars as far as the eye could see and he knew that the Porsches would be to his right.

'Hey Lenny,' a familiar voice shouted. It was Wally Jackson, wearing his trademark sheepskin coat, but today there was the addition of a furry Russian hat with the flaps pulled down over his ears. At the centre of the hat was the Red Star. 'What are you doing here two days on the trot?'

'I left my coat behind yesterday and I've just come to pick it up,' Lennie joked. 'Are you wearing that hat for a joke?'

'It was on sale. Russian hats are out of fashion apparently. I can't see why, they're very warm.'

'You're a dinosaur, Wally. You haven't seen any dodgy-looking blokes wearing Ray-Bans knocking about today, have you?'

'Not today but it's still early. There's time for them to turn up yet,' Wally joked. 'Seriously though, how did you get on with the police?'

'I had to go back to the Matrix unit this morning to meet with the Detective Inspector who is dealing with it, and we went back to the identification suite to see if they had mugshots of them,' Lenny explained. 'They have all Maddern's goons on file. It only took five minutes for them to find those two mugs from yesterday and they are in the system.'

'No surprise there,' Wally said.

'They are not long out from a fifteen-year stretch for holding up armoured vehicles. The detective said they were going to pick them up this afternoon and interview them for intimidating a witness and making threats to kill.'

'They both carry a few years,' Wally said, nodding.

'So, if they're at home when they knock on the door, they should be in the cells anytime soon.'

'You want to get them to charge them with slashing your tyres as well, at those prices,' Wally said. 'They were taking liberties with your lovely Jaguar and if they don't lock them up for that, then they won't lock them up for anything. Slashing the tyres on the car like that should bring a life sentence.'

'Do you know what,' Lenny said. 'I never even thought about my tyres when I was there this morning. They've done my head in so much I can't think straight but now you've mentioned it, I'm going to give the DI a ring and see what she thinks.'

'You should do. Don't let it go and you'll probably get some kind of compensation. What you've been through has got to be worth a few quid from his majesty's coffers, especially if a few of them get banged up for a long time. You will be doing us all a favour.'

Lenny and his friend walked around the vehicles that were coming up in the auction. They chatted about prices and all things to do with the selling cars business and nothing to do with the city's criminals. It was a nice feeling.

Lewis Cashman was standing on the pavement at the other side of the fence, watching them. His phone vibrated. A message from a client. They had an urgent job for him, but he had one of his own.

Chapter 26. Prison

'Fools, said I, 'You do not know, silence like a cancer grows...'

Adrian Norris was two years into a five-year sentence for grievous bodily harm. He'd gone to collect some money on a debt that he was owed, and the guy refused to pay and took a swing at him. Things had taken a turn for the worse and got a bit out of hand and Adrian put the guy in hospital.

He had been married to Heather Norris for eight years before they split up and were divorced. Adrian had been happy in the relationship in the early days, and they had four beautiful children, but he couldn't handle living with Heather's depressions and her mood swings. She seemed to be incapable of being happy. When he went to work, it was difficult to know which Heather he was going to come home to. Some days she would be happy, others almost euphoric, but most of the time she didn't even get out of bed, which had an impact on their children. He couldn't go to work and stay at work without wondering whether or not she had been shopping and made anything for the kids when they got home from school. Eventually he decided that enough was enough and he left, hoping that she would realise that she had to grow up and stand on her own two feet. Unfortunately, that's not the way it worked, and she latched on to a succession of losers for financial and emotional support. As long as they had some money, then nothing else seemed to matter. Adrian had tried to support her as much as possible financially, but she just threw it back in his face. The fridge and cupboards were still empty, the gas and electric were always running out, but Heather and whichever goon she was going out with at the time always had money for drink and drugs. In the end, he stopped giving her any money at all.

Adrian had been in the prison gym when he was given the news that his eldest daughter had been shot with an airgun. Needless to say, the news did not go down very well, and the lack of detailed information was making the situation worse. He had tried to speak to Heather but was unable to make contact and when he spoke to her mother, she told him, that David and Heather were being interviewed by the police in connection with the shooting. Adrian was beside himself at the thought that the guy his ex-wife was living with could be responsible for shooting his daughter in the face. If Adrian could have seen David at that point, he would have ripped his head from his shoulders.

Being behind bars when there are family emergencies on the outside, is the most frustrating thing that any parent could experience. The prison service has no sympathy for what is happening on the outside. Being separated from your family is part of the punishment. If you don't want to be away from your family when things go wrong, then don't get yourself sent to prison.

Adrian had managed to get hold of his mother, Joan, and he explained the situation to her. She said she would go to the Norris home, find out exactly what was going on and tell him later on that day. She told him not to worry, which was pointless. He was very worried.

Joan Norris had a reasonable relationship with Heather, purely and simply so that she could keep an eye on her grandchildren. It could be strained at times, especially when there was another man on the scene and Heather would make excuses for her not to come round and see the kids. Joan loved her grandchildren, and she was persistent. She was well aware of Heather and her moods, and she knew that they were the cause of the breakdown of her marriage to Adrian. There were times when she went to see the children, when they were so excited to go to McDonald's or Kentucky fried chicken, that they could hardly contain themselves. Joan knew that the kids were hungry a lot of the time and if she was going on a visit, she would make sure that she took a few bags of shopping with her. Milk, bread, cereal. Stuff they would eat for breakfast. Heather always said that there was no need to do that, as she was planning to go to the supermarket later that day, but Joan knew better.

The introduction of David Isle into her grandchildren's lives was never going to end well. From the first time that she met him, she knew that he was a wrong one. The man was arrogant and macho, and he wasn't good around the children. They were not his children and that was clearly obvious. The measure of his impact on the family was what her grandchildren thought of him, and they hated him. Especially Jacob. She shouldn't have a favourite grandchild, but Jacob was special to her. He reminded her of Adrian when he was a child.

Jacob had begun to act differently, especially when David was round. She knew that he wanted to talk to her and tell her something, but they just hadn't had the opportunity to talk in private. Now this dreadful thing had happened, and at first, she couldn't believe it for a second. Hope was such a beautiful human being. She mothered the other children as if they were her own, and she was twelve. This was her childhood too, and it was being stolen from her because her mother struggled to get out of bed. The fact that she had been shot and hospitalised was difficult to comprehend, and when she found out that David and Heather had been taken to the station to be interviewed, she could not believe what she was hearing.

She knew that social services were involved and that the children were on a child protection plan. That gave her some comfort to know that the professionals were overlooking what was going on in the family. She was a blood relative, the paternal grandmother, yet she had to tread very carefully around Heather and David. She knew that if she got on the wrong side of them, she would not be able to see her grandchildren as often as she would like.

Joan had received a call that day from the school, saying that Jacob was upset and that he wanted to see her. In the absence of his mother, Joan had gone to the school and taken Jacob home early. Obviously, Jacob had told his grandma everything that had gone on that morning. When he told her that David had said Hope deserved a 'fucking good hiding', she was speechless and concerned for the well-being of her grandchildren.

Jacob had said that the argument had started because there was no milk or bread, and that the cupboards were empty. There was nothing in for tea that night and Hope had told David that they needed to go shopping and David got angry.

Joan and Jacob went to the supermarket and spent an hour or so wandering around the aisles, chatting and buying all the stuff that the children didn't normally have. When they were finished, they had a trolley so full of goodies that Jacob said they could feed the whole street. Joan loaded up the car and they made their way back to the Norris home. She wasn't sure how well received she was going to be, under the circumstances. Whichever way you looked at it, it would appear that she was interfering, especially from David's perspective. She was the ex-husband's mother and had no place in his world.

Despite being Adrian's mother, she was their grandmother first and foremost and their safety was her concern, whether David liked it or not. She wasn't going to the house to stick her oar into what had happened, she was going there because Jacob had been upset at school and asked her to go there.

She hoped the shopping trolley full of groceries would be a peace offering, and they would understand that she meant well. She decided in advance not to mention what David had said to Hope that morning, it would be inflammatory no matter how she said it. There would be another time to address the issue. If Heather and David had been interviewed by the police in connection with the shooting, they would probably both be on the defensive and there was nothing to gain from causing an argument. She had also decided in advance not to tell Adrian what had been said. Her son was imprisoned for a violent crime and no matter how many times he explained the situation to her, she knew he was more than capable of becoming violent. There had been instances when he was a child where he lost his temper to the point that he had no control. As he became a teenager there were several examples of situations when walking away would have been the right thing to do, yet Adrian had chosen to stand and fight. While some might see this as an admirable thing to do, if the individual doesn't learn some control before adulthood, then prison is beckoning. She had no doubts in her mind that if she told him what David had said to Hope before she was shot, he would find a way to break out of prison and beat David to a pulp.

When Joan arrived at the house, there were still marked police cars parked along the street. She could see several uniformed officers knocking on doors around the estate, obviously canvassing for information about people owning airguns. Under the circumstances, people were more than happy to talk to the police. Anything to do with children being hurt and the public rallied to make sure that the perpetrators were brought to justice. The culture of never ratting to the police was overruled when children were involved. It was an unwritten rule that the majority of the public were more than happy to stick to.

Joan parked up and looked up at the house. There was a light on in the living room, and she could see the flickering colours of the reflection from the television on the walls. The children were all at school and Heather wasn't answering her phone, so she had to assume that it was David watching the television. She turned to

Jacob, and he was staring at the living-room window, a concerned expression on his face.

'Are you okay, Jacob?'

'I think David is at home in our house,' Jacob said pointing to the window. 'I don't want to talk to him. He's a prick.'

'I know what you think of David, and I'm not a big fan of his either, but calling him a prick isn't going to get us anywhere.'

'But he is a prick, and the police think that he shot Hope,' Jacob said, shaking his head.

'Now then, young man,' Joan said. 'If the police thought that David was responsible for shooting Hope, then I can tell you from experience that he would not be at home watching the television. They would have locked him up in a cell. There is absolutely no way they would have let that man out of the police station, if they thought he had shot your sister.' Jacob looked disappointed. 'I think the best thing to do is go inside and take the shopping with us, and we can put all that lovely food away in the fridge and in the cupboards. When your sisters get home, it will be a lovely surprise.'

'Okay, nan,' Jacob said, nodding. 'But he's still a prick.'

'You are growing up far too quickly for my liking, Jacob Norris, and you remind me all the world of your father. He was a stubborn little bundle of trouble when he was your age and there was no talking to him either. You will learn as you get older, that sometimes we have to bite our lip and keep what we really think locked away inside, where no one else can hear it. It causes less trouble that way.'

'Am I like my dad?' Jacob asked.

'You are like him in more ways than one.'

'When do you think my dad will be home?'

'Do you mean, when do I think will he be out of prison, because the two things are different,' Joan said. 'Your mum and dad aren't together anymore, and you know that, so when he does get out of prison and that should be soon, he will have to go and live in what is called a halfway house. I'm not sure where that will be, but he will have to stay there for about six months until he has met the terms of his release. He will be able to come and see you, but he won't ever come and live with you again.'

'I know that. I wish my mum would go away and then my dad could stay with us,' Jacob said, opening the door.

He slammed the door behind him, and Joan nodded and thought to herself that she wished that too, but it was never going to happen. She climbed out of the car and went to the boot, removing the bags. Jacob managed two and they walked to the front door. Joan opened the door and Jacob stepped inside. David met them in the hallway. His face showed disappointment.

'What are you doing here?' he asked.

'Jacob was upset at school, so I went to pick him up,' Joan said. 'We've been on a supply run on the way home. I thought you might need some food ready for the kids coming in from school.'

'We don't need your charity, thank you very much,' David said, shaking his head.

'It's not charity and it's not for you,' Joan said, angrily. 'So don't give me attitude. I'm here because my grandchildren are upset and hungry. That's what started the argument this morning, so if you don't like it, fuck off somewhere else!'

'You're a prick,' Jacob said, pushing past him with the shopping bags.

'Don't you speak to me like that,' David snapped. 'Cheeky little fucker.'

'Or what?' Jacob called from the kitchen. 'Will you shoot me in the face too?'

'Can you see what I have to put up with?' David asked, frustrated. 'I know you mean well and I'm sorry to be awkward but it's not easy being in a relationship when the children don't like me. It makes things very difficult.'

'You don't help yourself swearing at them, David,' Joan said. 'Calling Jacob a cheeky little fucker isn't going to endear him to you, is it?' David looked like a little boy lost. 'They're not adults, not like your mates in the pub where you can talk however you want to. They listen to your every word, and they will respond to whatever you say with similar. They're children.'

'I've never been around children before,' David said. 'I'm struggling with it.'

'And it shows,' Joan said. 'You need to build some bridges with them if you're serious about staying around.' He didn't reply. 'Are you serious about staying around?'

'I'm prepared to give it a try.'

'I'm going to make a spaghetti bolognaise for when they get back from school,' Joan said, calming down. 'Have you heard from Heather?'

'No.' David went back into the living room, sulkily.

'I'll get the other bags from the car,' Jacob said.

'I'll give you a hand,' David said. Jacob ignored him and walked down the path. He grabbed two more bags from the boot. David made sure he couldn't be seen from the house and grabbed the back of his jumper and twisted it hard. Jacob couldn't breathe.

'If you ever call me a prick again, I will hurt you like you've never been hurt before,' David whispered. 'I'll bury you in the ground and no one will ever know what happened to you, do you understand me, you little shit?'

Jacob nodded. David let go. Jacob ran up the path and looked back at David from the doorway. David was glaring at him. Joan was watching him from the kitchen window and the hairs on the back of her neck were standing on end. She could tell something had just happened, but she didn't know what.

Chapter 27. The Devil

FRANKIE WILLS WAS SITTING in his car waiting for his new boss to arrive. He had met Boothy on several occasions, mostly when Barry Maddern had overseen the outfit. Boothy had been in charge of supplying the younger outfits with ketamine and cocaine and he had done a very good job. The young criminals in and around the city looked up to Gary Booth as if he was some kind of fucking rock star, but that was before Maddern had snuffed it. Since Maddern had died, his status had gone off the chart. The chatter on the streets was that he was the main man now, and Frankie hadn't seen or heard of anybody that was going to challenge that perception. Frankie was more than happy that he was in charge because he had a decent relationship with him going back over a few years. They were roughly the same age and had come from the same background, which, Frankie thought, gave them a bond. He thought Boothy would be impressed with his operation.

Boothy was always positive and polite when he spoke to Frankie and Frankie was prepared to do pretty much anything that he asked as long as it stayed that way. His loyalty could never be questioned. He would go down for a life sentence before he would point the blame at the people above him. That was just the way things worked. In return, he wanted to be treated with respect, supplied with good quality merchandise, and paid a decent cut for the work that he did. That wasn't too much to ask for, in his opinion.

There had been times when Barry Maddern was in charge, that the temptation to turn and walk away from the outfit was overwhelming. Maddern and his lieutenants had got way above themselves, and a toxic culture of bullying, violence, and verbal abuse had developed. It had become entrenched in the people who ran the business. It appeared that being unreasonable and unnecessarily violent with their employees impressed the psychopath at the top of the tree. Frankie was no shrinking violet, and he was prone to take things too far at times, but he tried to talk to his employees the way he liked to be spoken to himself, as long as they did what they were told. He never talked down to them and he tried never to disrespect them in public. Yes, he fucked them and had a few blow jobs but that was part of the initiation. They were his and they enjoyed it. Some said they didn't, but he knew they did. He believed that to maintain the loyalty and respect of those closest to you, they must fear you. You are less likely to get stabbed in the back or grassed on, if the wheels came off. Respect others and they will respect you, but you must own them. That was the code that he convinced himself he worked by.

A new Range Rover Velar drove past him slowly. The alloy wheels had been sprayed matt black and the windows were tinted, so that it was almost impossible to see who the passengers in the vehicle were. It was Boothy. The vehicle stopped and Frankie got out of his car. He jogged over towards it, and opened the back door, climbing in while it was still crawling along the kerb. When he closed the door, the vehicle picked up speed and sped away from the meeting point. The driver was a black guy called Kirk. Frankie had met him a few times over the years, and he knew that he was old school and had been around longer than the Beatles. He had a fierce reputation and had worked on some of the most famous night clubs in the city. Despite being known as a hard man, Kirk was also a very popular member of the outfit. He never had a bad word to say about anybody, especially not behind their back. If he ever had a problem, it was dealt with face to face.

They drove in silence for about five minutes until they reached the huge roundabout at Tarbock Island. Kirk accelerated down the slip road onto the motorway and kept his eye on the rear view mirror to make sure that they weren't being followed.

'We're on our own,' Kirk said. 'Behind us is clear.'

'So, I hear you have had a bit of trouble with the residents in one of the blocks of flats,' Boothy said, half turning in his seat.

'Don't worry about it. It was nothing that I couldn't handle myself without bothering you and the other guys.'

'What happened?'

'It was just a couple of residents gobbing off, threatening to talk to the police when they were canvassing the estate.' Frankie explained. 'They said they were going to give them the names of some of the couriers I've been using. I had to warn them not to.'

'I need things to settle down very quickly. The police are nervous because of all the violence since Maddern snuffed it.'

'I'm on top of it.'

'You think so, do you?' Boothy asked, scowling. He didn't look happy.

'Yes. Is there a problem?' Frankie asked, confused.

'Yes, there's a problem. Putting members of the public into the hospital is the problem. Hurting the opposition is fine but not innocent bystanders.'

'I sent a message that needed to be heard,' Frankie said, offended.

'That's not my idea of running the business smoothly,' Boothy said, shaking his head. 'You need to get a grip of things sharpish and make sure the residents keep quiet, without putting any more of them into the back of an ambulance. Are we clear?'

There was venom in his words. Frankie was getting angry.

'It won't be necessary again,' Frankie said, feeling unappreciated. 'The job is done. Move on.'

'Don't tell me to move on, Frankie.'

'It's just a saying. No offence meant.'

'If you want to run that estate, you are going to be working in plain sight of everybody else who lives there; make enemies and you are going to get bubbled at every opportunity that arises.' Frankie felt like he was being told off by a teacher at school. 'Are you listening to what I'm saying?'

Frankie felt bitterly disappointed. He was convinced that he was going to get a pat on the back for the way he had dealt with the problem in the flats. It was clear that the new boss wanted things done with the least amount of attention. Frankie wanted to explain the situation and brag about the fact that they had a new flat to operate from but, under the circumstances, he decided not to tell him that an old woman had also been put into the back of an ambulance and would spend six weeks in the Royal. That wasn't going to go down well with the new regime.

'I've got everything under control. No one is going to say anything and no one else needs to get hurt.'

'Keep it that way.'

'We are ready to set up and get going again. I'm aiming to shift two and a half kilos a week plus a kilo of ketamine.'

'They are decent numbers and if you can do that under the radar, then there will be plenty of opportunities for you in the future. I am building this outfit up from the ground. Most of our best people are either dead or inside. It's a good opportunity to start from scratch and handpick the best people for the most important jobs.' Boothy thought for a moment. 'Where are you thinking of setting up the next operation from?'

'I'm not a hundred percent certain yet,' Frankie said, lying. 'But I've got my eyes on one or two locations. I want one where there is no chance of the police being involved in an eviction. There are a couple of cuckoo opportunities which we can keep quiet for a few months at least. Once I decide exactly which properties I'm going into, do you need to know where they are, or do you want me to just wing it?'

'Good question.' Boothy thought about it. 'I think it's probably better to leave you to your own devices. You know what you're doing, and you don't need me to micromanage your end of the operation.'

'Okay.' Frankie could sense that the borders had moved. Boothy had elevated himself way above where he had been before. His friend was gone, replaced by his superior.

'These are my rules. Don't cut my gear, sell it at a reasonable price, don't attract attention from the police to any parts of my business and I'll leave you to it. You can make a lot of money if you play your cards right.'

'Sounds like a good plan to me and I guarantee you that I won't let you down.'

'You will only let me down once. Let's put it that way.'

'I get the message loud and clear, boss,' Frankie said, feeling sick inside. He wanted to stab Boothy in the face. Arrogant cunt.

'I'm going to give you some advice that was given to me when I first started in this business as a teenager, and that is, respect your customers and the people who work for you. Don't fuck your staff. If you start hurting people, picking on little kids and old ladies, then you are going to have a very short career because people in this city won't stand by and watch the vulnerable be taken advantage of and bullied.'

'I understand exactly what you are saying, and I try and run the business along the same lines as you have laid out,' Frankie lied. He was thinking about the old lady who was lying in a hospital bed with a broken hip. He was thinking about buying breakfast, cigarettes and Russian vodka with her debit card. He was thinking about putting pressure on her for the pin number to her savings account. He was thinking about the little girl who had been taken from her school playground. He was thinking about how Andrew Head was squealing like a bitch when he fucked him on Mary's bed, and he was thinking about whether he was going to take the advice that he had just been given. He had a lot of time for Gary Booth once, but not now. It sounded like he had gone soft and was taking himself too seriously. It was as if he thought he was Robin Hood, taking from the rich and giving to the poor, except he was giving fuck all to anybody else but himself. He needed to have a good hard look in the mirror to see who was looking back at him, because he was hardly Bob Geldof.

'I work along the same principles as you do.' Frankie lied again. 'I think it's very important to look after the people who work for us and the community we work in. I've always said that if you make enemies in the local area, they will come back and bite you on the ass, at some point.'

'Good. Then we're on the same page.' Boothy signalled to head back and Kirk pulled off the motorway and drove onto the opposite carriageway. 'I'm glad we've had the opportunity to have this little talk. I think it's very important that I lay my stall out from day one, and then no one is under any illusions as to what is expected. Good to have you on board, Frankie,' Boothy said, but he didn't look him in the eye. 'I think we can build something together.'

Fifteen minutes later, Kirk pulled the Velar to a stop next to Frankie's vehicle. Frankie got out and closed the door. He made to shake his hand, but Boothy was looking in the opposite direction and left him hanging. Ignorant twat. Things were very different, and they weren't on the same page at all. Not by a long chalk. Frankie knew it was only a matter of time before they parted company, and he needed to line his pockets before they did. The Velar moved off.

'That man is full of shit. I'm hearing rumours that he's into young boys?' Boothy said, as they drove away.

'I'm hearing the same,' Kirk nodded in agreement.

'If he's a nonce, people will talk. We keep an eye on him and if he attracts any more attention, he's going for a swim.'

Chapter 28. Andy

ANDY WAS BEGINNING to panic. They had found his daughter's shoe and sock stuck in the railings which separated the school playground from the tree-lined road that led to the station. The only explanation which made any sense was that there had been a vehicle parked next to that spot. There was no way that two young girls could be bundled into a vehicle if it was further away. The risk of someone seeing the abduction was too great. He had said it to the lead detective, and he had agreed, but told him that that was only one possibility and he had to trust that they knew what they were doing.

Andy had told him about the altercation with the cuckoo in their building. He had explained what had happened to Sam and that he was in hospital as a result of the standoff. Andy told him, he was convinced this was connected. The detective said that he found it unlikely. He didn't offer an alternative motive for the abduction of his daughter and her friend. What other motives are there, except that some random pervert had been hovering around the schoolyard and abducted not one, but two children? It happens but how likely is that?

'Mr Topper?' A voice brought him back to reality. A detective approached. He looked to be in his twenties. 'We have some good news.'

'What is it?' Andy asked, his breath stuck in his chest.

'The girls have just walked into McDonalds in Huyton Village and asked for help,' the detective said. 'They're saying two men took them from the playground and then dropped them off in the restaurant car park. They gave them ten pounds to get some food.'

'This was a warning,' Andy said, looking to the lead detective as he approached. 'I told you what this was about. This is the dealer from my building telling me not to talk to you.'

'If it is, we'll nail the bastard,' the detective said. 'Don't worry. I'm not ignoring what you told me. Is there somewhere else you can stay for now?'

'Yes. We can go to my parents' home,' Andy said.

'Take your daughter there and I'll be in touch. We're not going to let this go, trust me.'

Chapter 29. Two days later

Sam was sitting up in his hospital bed watching visitors arrive on the ward. It was the highlight of the day, and it lifted the atmosphere amongst the patients. His injuries were beginning to heal, although his face still looked as if he'd been hit with a sledgehammer. The fracture to the back of his skull could be managed and it would heal by itself in time. The doctors had told him that he couldn't engage in anything like boxing or heading a football, not that he was likely to do either of those things. It did beg the question as to who would need to be given that advice, in the first place. If you went to a boxing club with a fractured skull, then you weren't right in the head. Another bang to the head was unlikely to make any difference.

Sam had been talking to Andy a lot on the phone and by text message and they were galvanised by their traumas. Andy had been through a nightmare when Lucy was taken from school, and he had been staying at his parents' house ever since. The sheer panic he had felt while Lucy was missing was debilitating. He said he had never experienced such helplessness. Earlier that morning, one of the nurses had brought him a message from Mary, who was being treated on another ward in the hospital. She had told him that she had broken her hip in a fall and wasn't able to walk. Sam had been shocked and dismayed at the news and asked the nurses if it was okay to go down and see her. They arranged for a porter to push him in a wheelchair because they still weren't happy with him walking too far, because of his head injury. When Sam got to the ward, Mary got very upset as she described what had happened to her. She told him that she had been attacked by some of the teenagers, who had been visiting their block of flats. She recognised one of them as Andrew Head. Sam was overwhelmed by her story and his anger had peaked at a level he had never felt before. It was one thing throwing a brick through his window, but kicking an old lady under a bus was just on another plane.

He had thought about what had caused this chain reaction of violence, while he was lying in his bed in the dark hours. The cuckoo had gone to extreme lengths to make sure that they didn't talk to the police. Sam and Mary were in hospital and Andy was at his parents' home. He hadn't gone back to his flat for fear of more reprisals against himself and his daughter. The situation was beyond the realms of reality for normal people. This was not the world that he wanted to live in. He was in no position to defend himself, Mary, Andy, Lucy or anybody else who lived in the building. A quick glance at his face would remind him of what happened the last time he decided to make a stand. It was a desperate situation, and he could see no solution to the problem. The strong were taking control of the weak. It seemed to be the story of the planet that they lived on. The weak are physically unable to resist the demands of the strong, without facing severe consequences. It was happening all over the world; Putin, with the nuclear might of Russia behind him, had invaded Ukraine and carried out horrendous attacks on the citizens of a peaceful country. Yet the world stood by and allowed it to happen because of his nuclear capability. Wasn't this exactly the same thing but on a smaller scale?

'Hello mate,' Andy said, as he approached his bed. 'I've brought you a couple of hot pies from the shop downstairs. How are you feeling today?'

'Thanks Andy, it's good to see you,' Sam said, sitting up in his bed. 'Thanks for the pies. They smell good. How is Lucy?'

'She's still very shaken and hasn't slept very well since she was taken. She keeps having nightmares and blames herself for talking to the man in the first place.'

'Poor little bugger,' Sam said, shaking his head. 'I can't believe these things have happened to us, it just all seems so ridiculously unnecessary. Have you seen Mary?'

'I called into her ward on the way up here, but they have taken her down to theatre. They are operating on her hip today and she will be down there for a few hours. I'll catch her tomorrow when she's awake.'

'She was really down in the dumps when I spoke to her. I think the attack has made her feel very vulnerable.'

'I feel the same way,' Andy said.

'She's always been a strong woman, able to defend herself and realising she was helpless has shaken her up badly,' Sam said, taking a bite from one of the pies. 'That is the best thing I have eaten in days.'

'Hello Sam, how's it going,' Carla said, approaching. She was wearing a white tracksuit and baseball cap, with a thick gold belcher chain around her neck. 'I can see you've got a visitor, sorry to interrupt, but I needed to come and speak to you about the money that you owe Frankie.'

'This is Carla, she works for Frankie, the cuckoo,' Sam said, turning to Andy. Andy looked shocked. 'This is my friend, Andy. Your friends took his daughter from her school.'

Andy's face turned to thunder, and he looked like he was about to explode. Sam had told Andy about his visit from the girl and the demand to pay back the money that the drug dealer had lost on the night he was attacked. Andy had been incensed by the story and had told Sam that he needed to go to the police. Sam said it wasn't an option. He didn't want to provoke any more violence.

'I don't know what you're talking about,' Carla said, chewing her gum with her mouth open. 'I don't have anything to do with any funny business. I just drive things here and there and take the odd message to people, like this one.'

'You're going to have to tell your friend that I haven't got the money yet.' Sam kept his voice low. He didn't want the other patients and visitors to hear. 'I've been in hospital the last few days, as he well knows, so I haven't had chance to arrange anything yet. You said Sunday.'

'Okay. I'll tell him that you can't pay it today but that means that he will probably put some interest on top. I don't think he will be very happy that you haven't made any effort at all,' Carla said, shaking her head. She pulled up a chair alongside the bed and sat next to Andy as if they were all best of friends. 'I am not looking forward to telling him you haven't got the money.'

'You people really do make me feel sick,' Andy said, astounded. 'How can you have the bare-faced cheek to come in here, demanding money and making threats? What the fuck is wrong with you?'

'I'm sorry. There's nothing wrong with me. We haven't met but it's obvious that you're a bit rude. I'm only here because I've been told to be here and you know the old saying, don't shoot the messenger.' Carla nudged him with her elbow, playfully. 'It's much better for me to come and ask for the money rather than Frankie Wills. He tends to bring a hammer.'

'What you are asking for is called receiving money with menaces,' Andy said. 'It's corruption, it's extortion, it's illegal and it's immoral.'

'Wow. They're big words for me. I wasn't too good at school. Can you say it in proper English, for me?'

'That doesn't surprise me one bit. Why don't your friends and this Frankie guy, get a job and go to work like the rest of us have to, rather than preying on people and stealing their money? You're a fucking disgrace and you should be ashamed of yourselves.'

'Oh, dear me. I do not like this guy one bit, Sam. He's very rude and I think he's a little bit jealous because my friend Frankie runs a very successful business,' Carla said, shaking her head. 'But that's understandable.'

'You are unbelievable.' Andy said, reaching boiling point. 'I should throw you through the window.'

'I would slit your throat before you moved more than a few steps.' Carla showed the handle of a box-cutter and grinned. 'If you fancy a few stripes on your face, go for it.'

'You're carrying a blade in a hospital and making threats,' Andy said. 'You're not very bright, are you?'

'Call the police if you like,' Carla whispered. 'But dropping your kid off at school might become a bit of a worry for you. Better to keep your gob shut, know what I mean?' She put her finger to her lips and shushed him.

'Very brave,' Andy said. 'She's six, for fuck's sake.'

'I don't really care what this guy thinks and I'm only here to pass on a message, but I think it's only fair to let you know how these things work,' Carla said, leaning forward and lowering her voice. 'You see you're in here, and my friends are out there. You owe them money and you're saying that you can't pay it back. Usually what happens is, my friends would go to the property of the person who owes them money, and they take goods to the value of the amount owed.' Carla paused. 'That is just how it works and if there isn't enough in the property to balance the account, then it will be deducted from the debt owed and you will still have to pay the remaining amount before Sunday.'

'Look Carla,' Sam said. 'I've told you that I don't have the money right now, but I will try and get it together before Sunday. It doesn't matter how many times you come in here making your veiled threats. I can't magic the money out of thin air. I just don't have it.'

'Okay. It's your funeral.'

'How much are you saying that he owes to these gangsters?' Andy asked, fuming now.

'One thousand five hundred pounds,' Carla said, her voice a whisper. 'I don't want to embarrass Sam by letting the whole world know that he owes money. There is no need to embarrass him.'

'Fucking hell, you're a special kind of nutcase,' Andy said, shaking his head. 'I'm not sure where they find you people, but it amazes me how you seem to find each other.'

'Birds of a feather, flock together,' Carla said, smiling. She made claws with her hands. 'But we're birds of prey.'

'Tell me where to drop the cash off and I will be there in an hour. Make it somewhere public.'

'No Andy,' Sam said, becoming agitated. 'I'm not having you paying this debt for me. It's my own fault and I'm going to have to deal with it myself.'

'Unless you find a money tree between now and Sunday, you're not going to be able to pay this twat what he wants. We both know how this goes when you can't pay. They just pick another figure and double it and the amount goes up and up to the point where you will never be able to pay them off. They will be on your back forever.' Sam nodded.

'I'll pay you back.'

'Where and when?' Andy said.

'I'll be at the front entrance in an hour and a half,' Carla said, smiling. 'Will that be enough time for you to go to the bank and take the money out?'

'I will see you there in an hour and a half,' Andy said. 'And once the money is paid, don't even think about coming back to ask for more. I understand that the dealer lost money that night, I'll pay the debt and then we are done with it.'

'You have a very good friend there, Sam. even if he is rude. I don't know many people who would put their hand in their pocket like that to pay someone else's debt.'

'It just goes to show that there are some decent people around. I guess you just don't get to meet many of them in your line of work,' Sam said.

'Ta ta for now,' Carla said, leaving with a spring in her step. 'See you soon Andy, don't be late.'

And with that, she was gone. The two men sat in silence for a few moments, while they digested what had just happened. It was difficult to comprehend how the criminal world could just exist without reproach. Carla could walk around in her expensive clothes, wearing her expensive jewellery with a smile on her face, and nobody was any the wiser what she was up to.

'I'm trying to get my head around what has just happened and where this ends,' Andy said, shaking his head. 'If I meet her and give her the money, do you believe that that will be the end of the matter?' Sam didn't reply. 'I'm not sure that these people are going to let you off the hook so easily. It would be simple for them to say, hold on a minute, you actually owe us double that, and we need it by next Wednesday. They can say what the fuck they like if you keep on paying them.'

'Don't say that. I don't think I can cope with this any longer. I really am beginning to lose my marbles with the whole thing,' Sam said. 'Do you really think they will ask for more?'

'Yes, I do think that,' Andy said. 'Put yourself in their shoes for a moment. They have told you that you owe them money, which you don't, but you're going to pay it anyway.' Sam thought about it. And he thought that Andy had a very valid point. If he was prepared to pay the money they had asked for, then why not ask for more? It made perfect sense. Sam had already demonstrated his reluctance to become embroiled in another standoff against Frankie Wills and his outfit, so what was he likely to say if they demanded more money?

Sam felt like he was backed into a corner and there was no way out. It was like being in a dark hole, looking up at the light but not being able to climb out. It was a desperate place to be, but the strong prey on the desperate people in our communities.

'I don't want you to give them money if they're going to ask for more and you're right, why wouldn't they ask for more?' Sam said. Tears formed in his eyes, and one trickled down his left cheek. He wiped it away with the back of his hand, embarrassed and ashamed of himself. 'I was in pain, and I was frightened, and I didn't know what else to say. I should never have agreed to pay them that money. I wasn't thinking straight, and I thought it would get them off my back but that's not the way this works, is it?'

'No. That isn't the way this works,' Andy said, pulling his chair closer to the bed so that no one could hear their conversation. 'You need to understand that we are in this together. They hurt you, they've hurt Mary, and they kidnapped my daughter from a playground, just to send a message. Can you imagine what they will do if they say you owe them money and you don't pay it?

'I can't see a way out. There isn't anything that they won't do to get what they want,' Sam said. 'My mind is completely blank, and I just can't see a way out of this, but if you've got any ideas, I'm more than ready to listen to them.'

'The detective who came to Lucy's school has kept in touch and they've been looking into Frankie Wills and his operations on our estate,' Andy said. 'He couldn't say too much for obvious reasons, but he gave me the impression that Frankie is already under the microscope. I don't know what that means exactly, but he said if anything else happened, no matter how trivial it may seem, I have to phone him and let him know. He said it could be the straw that breaks the camel's back.'

'What do you think he means by that?' Sam asked.

'I think maybe they have him under observation and are already building a case against him. They could be looking for some final pieces of the jigsaw, so that they can put him back in his box for good.'

'I think I get what you are saying,' Sam said. 'Are you suggesting that we go to the police with this, right now?'

'Yes,' Andy said. 'That girl is waltzing around making threats with a Stanley knife in her pocket. She needs locking up along with the rest of them. If I make a call and tell the police that they are demanding money with menaces, and that they are insisting I meet them in the foyer of the hospital with a large sum of cash to pay a debt which doesn't exist, they might jump on it.'

'What if they don't?'

'Then we haven't lost anything and we're still in the same situation that we're in right now,' Andy said. 'I don't think that we can deal with this alone. We need the police to sort these bastards out, because we can't do it. I don't want to go back to my flat, and be looking over my shoulder every time I take Lucy to school. These people need to be taken off the streets.'

'I agree with you but I'm worried that it might create a worse reaction than we've had already,' Sam said.

'How can it be any worse?' Andy asked.

Sam wasn't certain that the decision they were making was the right one, but he was certain that it wasn't the wrong one. Giving Carla one thousand five hundred pounds for an imaginary debt, was likely to drag him deeper into the clutches of a violent organised criminal gang. He would be indebted to them, here ever after, and they would never let him go. It was a huge gamble but one he was prepared to take. It was time to take a stand.

'Do it,' Sam said. 'Make the call.'

Chapter 30. The Devil

Up ahead in the distance, I saw a shimmering light, my head grew heavy, and my sight grew dim...

FRANKIE WILLS WAS SITTING on the settee in Mary's flat watching daytime television. He was drinking a bloody Mary, which he thought was very apt considering where they were now running the business from. They had the keys to her front door and the keys to the communal door. It could not have been simpler. The other residents in the building appeared to be completely unaware that Mary wasn't at home. The other residents who had caused a problem, Sam and Andy, were not at home either. Sam was still in hospital and would be for at least another few days and Andy had not come back to his flat since he was sent a warning. Everything was about as perfect as it could be, but Frankie had learned a lesson from the way he had operated in the flat across the hallway. Customers coming and going through the foyer of the building was always going to attract attention and he should have known better. It was better to operate with a bit more subtlety.

Mary's flat was at the back of the building, which overlooked a grassy area, and the footpath which led through the other blocks of flats to the rest of the estate. She had two bedrooms, one was being used by Frankie when he stayed over or Carla sometimes, when she was left in charge. The second bedroom had a window which opened onto the grassy area, and it was ideal for serving up product without being seen by the rest of the residents. Customers and couriers could come and go on their bikes and scooters and simply knock on the window to order their drugs. His couriers could knock on the window and drop off their takings without ever entering the building. It was the perfect setup and he intended to use it for as long as he possibly could. He was hoping Mary would stay in hospital for a few months. That would be ideal. It would give him enough time to build up a bank, so that he could go it alone. It had only been a few days, but the operation was running like clockwork, and he had the added bonus of using Mary's debit card for alcohol and cigarettes. He had considered sending Carla to see her in hospital but was wary of what Gary Booth had said to him. Putting pressure on an old woman would be frowned upon by the local community. He didn't think that Mary would be in the frame of mind to talk to the police, but you never could tell. Some people are very stubborn and will never listen to reason, no matter how painful reason is. It was better to leave her be for now. Business was good.

Frankie got up and went into the kitchen to top up his drink. He heard a knock on the bedroom window and then the voices of his cuckoos talking to the customer through the window. The transaction was over in less than thirty seconds, and he watched a teenager crossing the grassy area on his BMX bike. It was simple and it was safe for now. He filled his glass half full of vodka and topped it up with tomato juice and a splash of Worcester sauce. A couple of ice cubes from the freezer completed his cocktail. He wanted to stir it and opened one of the drawers in the kitchen. It was full of bills and letters and there were two small notebooks with pens fastened to them with elastic bands. He closed the drawer and moved to the next one, opening it. It was the cutlery drawer. A light bulb switched on in his brain and he went back to the previous drawer and opened it again. He took out the notebooks and removed the elastic bands, flicking through the pages with his fingers. The first page of the second notebook that he opened had a list of all Mary's passwords and pin numbers. He smiled to himself and sipped his cocktail. Now he had access to her savings account too. There would be no need to pay her a visit in hospital anymore. He had everything he needed for a profitable stay.

Chapter 31. Carla

Then she lit up a candle, and she showed me the way...

CARLA HAD BEEN ON THE phone for the best part of forty minutes, setting up the collection of the debt owed by Sam. He was a first-class chump and a real wimp, and he deserved to be robbed. Frankie had left the arrangements to her. When she spoke to him on the phone, she could hear a slight slurring in his voice. He had probably been on the vodka since silly o'clock that morning. There was a pattern forming in Frankie's routine, and vodka was becoming a major part of his diet. Not that there was anything wrong with drinking vodka but drinking it all day will affect your judgement. Frankie's judgement had been questionable for the last few months. He had become irrational, unreasonable, and prone to violent outbursts. Carla knew that Frankie had a thing for her and when he was drunk, he was a letch and he would try it on, but she never let him get past first base. The most he got was a hand job. Not only was he too old for her, but she didn't want a boyfriend who wanted teenage boys. Plus, he was likely to beat her up on a regular basis. She had more than a few friends who had fallen into that trap already and they were still teenagers.

Frankie had told her to squeeze Sam for a few grand and tell him that it was for loss of earnings. She had been flexible with the amount because she realised he was more likely to pay without kicking up a fuss. If the demand had been too high, then he was more likely to go to the police as there would be no other solution for him. She hadn't been greedy, and it had paid off. His friend Andy was a complete knobhead, but he had been willing to bail his friend out by paying the debt. That was a really nice thing to do but it was also a very stupid thing to do. Carla had arranged for a couple of Frankie's outfit to be at the hospital when Andy arrived with the money. Andrew Head had refused at first, but Carla said she would tell Frankie and he changed his tune. Another three teenagers were waiting on the car park for Andy to arrive. The plan was to attack him as soon as he left his vehicle, steal the money and give him a good kicking. This plan had two advantages; one, the debt would still be owed because the money had never reached Carla, and two it would put Sam and Andy in their place. Anyone who thought they could dictate the terms of a debt owed to Frankie, or the outfit, didn't understand how business worked. The outfit would tell them when the debt was paid. People like Andy thought they could just throw some cash around and everyone would go away and leave him alone. He was delusional and he was about to learn a very harsh lesson. It was a lesson that he would never forget. Frankie wasn't the type of man to forgive and forget, and the residents of the flats would rue the day that they had chosen to stand up to him. There was no standing up to Frankie and that would become clear today.

Carla was in the foyer of the hospital, sipping a latte and checking her Instagram account. She didn't use it to post pictures, but it was useful for sending and receiving messages instead of using a text. Text messages can be intercepted in several different ways without the sender or receiver being aware that their conversations were being monitored. Encrypted phones were all the rage for a while, but nowadays they were an admission that you were involved in criminal activity. Anybody using an encrypted phone is up to no good. There was a vibration on her phone, and she went to her WhatsApp messages. The message was from Andrew Head. Andy had parked at the far side of the car park. He was sitting in his van.

She checked her watch, and he was 10 minutes early. That was good. This was going to be one of the easiest paydays she had ever had, and it would be a gift which never stopped giving. The debt would still be owed, and Sam would have to pay it again. She smiled and walked to the window to watch the sharks circle and attack. Andy wouldn't know what had hit him.

Andy zipped up his coat pocket and opened the door, climbing out of the van into the cold wind and rain. It was a grey day. He was feeling anxious as he locked the van and walked away. The incident at his daughter's school had sent him reeling and his sense of injustice was off the scale. There were no words to describe how angry he felt that anybody would think it was okay to use his daughter as a pawn in a deadly game. Any father would feel the same way. He would die to protect his child.

As he walked away from the van, he scanned the car park from left to right. It was absolutely packed and there were hardly any spaces. The payment machines were nothing more than rusted pieces of metal, bent and twisted, no longer used but not removed. The payment was done by contactless card at a unit in the foyer of the hospital. He made his way between the vehicles and caught sight of a teenager wearing a dark tracksuit, weaving between the cars to his left. He was three rows away. To his right he saw another tracksuit-clad youngster, this one riding an electric scooter. His nerves began to jangle, and his heartbeat quickened. This was one of the scenarios he had feared. Carla was not a human being to be trusted and he was going to arrive at the hospital with a large sum of money in his pocket. It was a perfect opportunity to hijack the payoff and claim that it was somebody else's responsibility. That way they could keep Sam on the hook and bleed him dry. He heard footsteps to his right and turned around to see a youth wearing a scarf across his face and a hood on his head. The eyes were recognisable, they were familiar, but he couldn't put his finger on who it was. He put his head down and walked quickly switching from one row to another, walking past two cars and then switching back again. His slalom between the vehicles was buying him precious time and putting yards between himself and his pursuers. He wasn't certain that they were pursuing him, but his instincts told him they were. Andy broke into a jog and made a beeline for the main entrance of the hospital. He was 200 yards away. There was a line of ambulances to his left and a zebra crossing to his right. There was a crowd of people waiting at the zebra, so he decided to cross the road immediately, and use the ambulances as a shield. As he crossed the road, the youth on the electric scooter used the opportunity to accelerate to top speed. He was aiming directly at Andy and there was nowhere for him to go. It seemed that a full-on collision with the electric bike was inevitable. One of the ambulance men ran towards him and Andy was confused. He didn't understand what he was doing. The electric scooter was simply yards away when the ambulance man launched himself in a death-defying rugby tackle, which took the rider off the scooter and took him to the ground with a painful crunch. Other people wearing ambulance uniforms ran across the road and took the BMX riders off their bikes and bundled them to the ground where they were cuffed.

Inside the foyer, Carla was watching the action through the window, her mouth opened in surprise. She couldn't fathom why her associates were being tackled to the ground. It was excessive force to say the least, she thought. Why they were getting involved was beyond her.

'Carla Samson, you're under arrest for demanding money with menaces and carrying a concealed weapon,' a voice said. 'You do not have to say anything...'

Carla was read her rights and put into the back of a police van along with her colleagues. Andy walked into the reception area alone and waited at the entrance to the Costa. Detective Jack Roman approached him.

'Well done, Andy,' the detective said. 'You and your friend should be proud of yourselves. It's about time people stood up to these scumbags.'

'Anything we can do, we will,' Andy said.

'I need you to let us go to your flat tomorrow and put some cameras in your windows. There's activity that we need to record. No questions asked. In and out, okay?'

'Okay.'

'You need to stay away for now, right?'

'Right.'

Chapter 32. Two Weeks Later

Some dance to remember, some dance to forget...

DETECTIVE CHIEF INSPECTOR French was holding a briefing with the team investigating the OCG crisis in the city. It was like a spider's web which spread across the city and trying to unravel it was proving challenging. The Anthony Head murder had become a red herring, and this had complicated their investigation. The original information about the storage unit in Warrington had come from an anonymous tip off, which could only have been made by someone close to the organisation. Everyone they had interviewed denied any knowledge of the body in the freezer and the mysterious trunk which had been removed.

'We have a statement from the manager of the Storage King facility in Warrington,' French said to his detectives. 'He has changed his original statement, stating that he had been intimidated by Gary Booth. We all know Booth and he is a very intimidating character, so it doesn't take much of a stretch of the imagination to take Rupert Stokes at his word.' He changed the image on the screen and DI Evans took over.

'We have the statement from Stokes, which is backed up by one of his employees, who was working on the reception the day that the trunk was removed. His description of the man who took the trunk fits that of Gary Booth. But I have to ask you all this question: the anonymous tip off came the day after Booth had been into that unit. Stokes claims that the same man he saw removing the trunk paid for that unit with a prepaid MasterCard. If this is true, why would Gary Booth make an anonymous call to tip us off about a body which only he could have put there?' Chatter spread across the gathering. He waited for the room to settle. 'It doesn't add up to me. We have interviewed Booth, and he made a no comment interview. He didn't answer a single question.'

'How do we know that the tip off was made by Booth?' a detective asked.

'We don't. But if he did make the anonymous phone call, then his motive for doing so would be for that body to be discovered. He wanted us to find that body, but why?'

'Because he wanted to implicate somebody in the murder,' another detective said.

'Exactly my thoughts,' French said. 'Let's assume for one minute that somebody else rented that unit and stashed a body in it along with a trunk full of an unknown valuable hoard. It could be cash, it could be drugs, it could be weapons, but we can safely assume that it's valuable. We know Gary Booth went into that unit, that is a fact. And we know he removed the trunk. On the assumption whoever actually rented the unit is pissed off that his valuables have been removed, and a murder victim discovered, what would be the best way of turning the tables?'

'Get a witness to say that Booth rented the unit in the first place,' Talbot said.

'Absolutely that would be the best way and what we have now is a case that can swing both ways on the testimony of one man,' French said. He nodded to Evans to continue.

'Stokes had an appointment to talk to us about his finances around the time that the unit was rented. When we arrived at his home his car was gone, the back door was open, and there was blood on the floor. It had all the signs of an abduction. When we caught up with Stokes, he said that he had had a fall and broken his nose on the door frame of the back door. I know a liar when I see one, and he is a liar. His bank account showed a lack of activity for three to four months following the rental of that unit. He hardly withdrew any money from his account, which means he was in possession of a large amount of cash, and that was funding his lifestyle. When we pressed him about the cash, he admitted to coming into a large sum of money from a win on a racehorse. The time and date of the race is genuine. It was a horse called Superpower which came in at twenty to one at Chepstow. Unfortunately, the bookmaker sold his property, and it was subsequently demolished along with the row of shops, and Mr Corbett himself died three months after closing the shop. So, we have a man who could have taken a bribe, who has manufactured a very clever way to explain where the money came from.'

'We can't identify who gave him the cash,' Talbot said. 'There is no way to trace it.'

'If Rupert Stokes was taken from his home and persuaded to change his statement to make Gary booth look guilty of murder, then he is in grave danger. We will have to offer him witness protection, if he wants to survive much longer.'

'Whoever rented that unit could have put pressure on Stokes to point the finger of blame at Gary Booth. He has changed his statement. We have a corroborating witness, who will stand up in court, but in my opinion, whoever killed Anthony Head, is going to get away with it unless we can find evidence to prove otherwise.'

Chapter 33. Heather

And she said, "We are all just prisoners here, of our own device"...

THE SITUATION AT THE Norris home hadn't got any better. Heather had come home from the hospital each day a little bit more despondent and more depressed than usual. Hope wasn't responding and their situation was dire. There were no medicines that they could give her to make her better. The damage was deep inside her skull where it couldn't be reached, and the doctors said they would keep her sedated so that Hope could fight.

The family was falling apart and every day there was a trauma between the kids and David. David had become defensive and aggressive and the kids were being awkward and refusing to acknowledge that he was even in the same room as them. Jacob had been especially quiet, and the school had noticed some bruises on his arms and legs, which they had spoken to social services about. Their social worker Phil had been on the phone daily and he was being even more of a pain in the arse than he normally was. Her ex-husband Adrian was on the warpath, threatening David at every opportunity. David wasn't helping the situation. He kept swearing at the kids, which was driving Heather around the bend. She felt like she couldn't get a minute's peace because of the constant bickering between her children and her partner. Her ex-mother-in-law Joan had been a diamond. She was taking Heather to the hospital every day as well as helping them out with food for the kids.

There was a knock on the front door and Heather closed her eyes and took a deep breath. Phil had said he would be there before dinner time, but it was nowhere near yet. It was too early for Joan to be here to take her to the hospital and they didn't have any random callers at the house. She opened the door and was surprised to see Detective Inspector Bennett standing there with a uniformed officer.

'What are you doing here?' Heather asked.

'I'm arresting you for grievous bodily harm, Heather.' The uniformed officer put handcuffs on her.

'Again!' Heather protested. 'This is going beyond a joke. I've told you what happened, and I can't see why you're arresting me again. What is going on?'

'We can explain everything to you at the station when you have legal representation,' Jane said, stepping inside the house. 'Where is David?'

'He's gone to the bookmakers to put some bets on horses,' Heather said.

'He's got money for gambling then?'

'Actually, he's very good with horses, he's been winning quite a lot lately,' Heather said, struggling. 'This is a total waste of time and I'm going to put a complaint in.'

'You can do all the complaining that you like but if I was you, I would be using the time between here and the station to get your story straight, because you are in big trouble, lady.'

Chapter 34. David

Last thing I remember, I was running for the door, I had to find the passage back, to the place I was before...

DAVID WAS STANDING next to the roulette machine in the bookies, pumping the slot with pound coins. It was close to paying out and he could sense a big win was on the cards. Having said that, he had the same feeling the day before but lost over seventy pounds. A man in his fifties came and stood next to him and pointed to one of the reels.

'I would put a tenner on that one,' he said.

David looked around to make sure no one was watching and slipped his hand into his pocket. He took out a 10-pound wrap and handed it to the man, who swapped it for a 10-pound note. David slipped the note into his inside pocket next to the others. He had been selling wraps of whiz for Frankie Wills for a couple of months now. David had problems with amphetamine abuse which made his mood swings erratic. In past relationships, it had caused him to be violent and unstable. It was easier to work for Frankie and make a few quid on the side. This way he could have as much amphetamine as he wanted and have money to buy a bit of weed and some vodka for Heather and himself to enjoy at night time when the little brats had finally gone to bed. He heard the door open and saw uniforms in the reflection of the machine. His heart was thumping in his chest because of the wraps that he had in his pocket and the amount of cash he was carrying. If they were here for him, he was busted. That fucking social worker would be over the moon if he got done for possession.

'David Isle,' a female voice said. 'I'm arresting you for grievous bodily harm. You don't have to say anything but anything you do say...'

David didn't hear the rest of what the police detective was saying. He was far more concerned about the fact that he was being rearrested for the assault on Hope. He knew the way the police worked, and they didn't arrest people unless something had changed. They obviously had some new evidence.

Chapter 35. The Para

You can check out any time you like, but you can never leave...

JERRY SAMSON WASN'T a happy man. His sister, Carla, had been remanded in custody, without bail, and sent to Styal prison. It was an all-female prison near Stoke and she had cried in the dock when the judge sent her down. She had been a ticking time bomb since hanging around with that cunt, Frankie Wills. He had warned her to stay away from Frankie but talking to Carla was like talking to a brick wall. She was like all teenagers of that age, they think they know it all, when they know fuck all. It had been a bit of fun at first. She was hanging out with Frankie and his teenage couriers, drinking shots and smoking a bit of weed but he could see the writing on the wall very quickly. Frankie Wills had a thing for teenage girls and teenage boys. Why else would he surround himself with them?

There were no grown men or women in Frankie Will's outfit, which was concerning to Jerry. The shot drinking and weed smoking was the bait that Frankie laid to attract new employees, teenagers that he could prey on in more ways than one. Rumours had it that Frankie was a nonce. Jerry had asked Carla if Frankie had propositioned her for sex and she said that he had tried it on when he was pissed, but she had handled it and didn't need him to interfere. Jerry had decided to take a step back and let her make her own mistakes; with hindsight that was a mistake in itself. After a short time of letting the new recruits become comfortable, Frankie would tell them that they had to contribute to the cost of the vodka and the cannabis that they had consumed. Obviously, this would come as a shock to most of these youngsters and they had no money. At this point, Frankie would spring the trap and tell them that they could pay off their debts by becoming a courier for him. Once they had broken the law and carried drugs for him, he had his hooks into them. Of course, he would tell them that they could pay their debts off with a couple of blowjobs or a fuck. Jerry had heard it from several sources that Frankie was a wrong one. He was also a psychopath with a vicious temper. Carla had told Jerry that he had cuckooed some flats in the next street and had a run in with some of the residents. A bloke was in hospital with a fractured skull and an old lady had her hip broken, and to top it off, he had kidnapped a six-year-old from a school playground. This guy might have thought he was made from asbestos, fireproof and indestructible, but he wasn't. Jerry had watched his mum and dad crumble in the courtroom as his sister was led away. Carla was a liability to herself but there was only one person to blame for her being in prison. Frankie Wills.

Chapter 36. Heather

And it's been the ruin of many a poor boy, and God I know I'm one...

HOWELL JONES WAS SITTING next to Heather in the interview room waiting for DI Bennett to arrive. The circumstances of the case had changed dramatically, and both suspects would have to be kept apart and represented by different solicitors. There was a potential for both suspects to point the finger at each other to cast reasonable doubt on their own situation. Despite being a couple, things could get tricky very quickly. The detectives walked into the room and the introductions were made for the benefit of the recording.

'I want to just recap exactly what you said at your first interview,' Jane said. 'You said that you were in bed asleep and only remember waking up when Jacob ran back into the house and said that something had happened to Hope. Is that correct?'

'If you say it, is I can't remember,' Heather said. 'I don't know why we have to go over all this again. It's like going round in a circle and it's making me dizzy.'

'I'll tell you why you are here. We have had some of the forensic test results back and they are very interesting,' Jane said, looking at the screen on her laptop. 'You said that David never took the gun from the wardrobe and that you've never touched it. Is that correct?'

'If you say it is. I can't remember,' Heather said. She twiddled her thumbs and couldn't make eye contact with Jane. 'If my daughter had been shot in the face and I had touched the gun, then I would remember,' Jane added.

'I don't know what you're talking about. You're talking gobbledygook.'

'We have your prints on the gun.'

'I don't know how that could have happened,' Heather said. 'I've never touched that gun. Maybe I've moved it sometime when I've been getting clothes out of the wardrobe. That's the only way you could have my fingerprints on it.'

'We have your DNA on it as well,' Jane said.

'Like I said I may have brushed it or moved it without realising when I've been looking for clothes,' Heather said. She was stumbling, her words confused.

'That won't explain your fingerprints and DNA being on the gun because we found them on the inside of the gun, which means the barrel of the gun was broken ready to be loaded.'

'Can you be more specific, for my benefit please?' Howell asked.

'Yes of course.' Jane turned the laptop round and showed the image of a meteor 22 air rifle. It had been broken at the centre so that a pellet could be loaded into the barrel and so that the piston is forced back under extreme pressure. When the trigger is pulled the piston is released and the projectile is fired. 'This is how the gun looks when it is being loaded. The pellet is held between the forefinger and the thumb and pushed into the barrel using the thumb. We have a partial thumbprint and her DNA on this part of the barrel. We also have her skin at the base of the pellet where she has pushed it into the barrel.' Howell removed his glasses and looked at his client. 'There is nothing you can say that explains your thumb print and skin being on the barrel of the gun, and on the base of the pellet that was removed from your daughter's head. The only explanation for it, is that you loaded that rifle before it was fired.'

'I didn't shoot my daughter!' Heather snapped. She put her head in her hands and sobbed.

'I'm going to suggest that under the circumstances we take a break so that I can talk to my client and give her my best advice,' Howell said. Jane looked annoyed. 'Otherwise, I'm going to advise her to make no comment from now on. There is nothing that she can say which will not be incriminating. I'm sure you can see how precarious her situation is. There may be an explanation as to how this forensic evidence has been found where it is, but I insist on talking to my client about this before she incriminates herself any further.'

'Okay. You can have half an hour with her,' Jane suggested.

'Let's make it an hour and if we could have some cold water and two cups of coffee that would be ideal,' Howell said.

Chapter 37. David

S uch are promises, All lies and just what a man wants to hear, he hears what he wants to hear, and disregards the rest...

DAVID ISLE WAS WAITING nervously to be interviewed. He had been arrested in the bookmakers and searched when he arrived at the custody suite. The police found nine small wraps of amphetamine and a small amount of cash, which was evidence enough of him dealing. As if things weren't bad enough already, the final nail in the coffin of his relationship had just been hammered home. The lanky twat from social services would be jumping for joy when he found out. That was more annoying than anything a judge could do. He had been talking to a duty solicitor who was willing to take his case but said they would sit in on the interview until a permanent representation could be found. David wasn't really that bothered who represented him because he thought that he was quite capable of representing himself. The door opened and the duty solicitor walked in. She was Carol Miller and she looked like she had just finished university, too young and too trendy to be a decent brief, but she smelled good, and he would give her one. Always look on the bright side of life, David thought to himself.

Detective Inspector Bennett came into the room with the black detective who had interviewed him before. He liked her, she was fit. David smiled at them as they sat down, as if they were old pals getting back together again. He couldn't get to grips with the gravity of the situation. People seem to be making a mountain out of a molehill. Jane went through the formalities for the recording and paused to look at something on her laptop, which David thought was rude.

'I'm just going to come straight to the point, as there is no point in dancing around the details,' Jane said. 'We have had forensic results back from the lab and your fingerprints are on the butt and the handle of the gun and your forefinger print is on the trigger.'

'Is that it?' David said, laughing. 'Of course my fingerprints are on my gun because it's my gun. Why wouldn't they be on it?'

'Ordinarily, I would take that as a reasonable answer, however we have also found a thumbprint inside the barrel of the gun, which belongs to Heather, and there are traces of her skin at the base of the pellet which was removed from Hope's head.' David looked down at the table and it was obvious that the cogs were turning in his brain, trying desperately to come up with an explanation that would match the forensic evidence. 'Before you say anything let me tell you how I see it. The forensic evidence tells me that Heather loaded the gun. She put the pellet into the barrel, and she pushed it into place with her thumb. But she didn't fire the gun because it's your print on the trigger.'

'But it's my gun, so my prints will be on it.' David said sulkily. His shoulders seemed to shrink, and he sunk down in his chair, a sign that he couldn't wriggle out of it. 'I don't know why Heather's fingerprints are on the barrel. That's a bit of a mystery, and I can't explain it.'

'But it isn't a mystery, David. The pellet that was removed from Hope's head has traces of Heather's skin on it. She pushed that projectile into the barrel of your gun, and your fingerprint is on the trigger, which means you fired it.'

The solicitor twisted uncomfortably in her chair. The expression on her face was one of distaste. She didn't want to be there sitting next to a man who had fired an air rifle at a child. The evidence was clear and irrefutable.

'My advice to you in light of this evidence would be to tell the truth or say nothing,' she said to him without looking at him.

David sighed heavily and put his head back against the chair, staring at the ceiling with a smile on his face. He shook his head and laughed to himself.

'I'm not sure which part of this you find funny,' Jane said shaking her head. 'If I was you, I would take your solicitor's advice and tell the truth. This is your one and only opportunity to tell us what happened. If you don't tell us the truth you are going to get buried in court and that won't go well for you when it comes to sentencing.'

David sat up and coughed into his hand. He looked at the detectives with a grin on his face.

'I am not going to lie to you, you've done a good job there,' David nodded. 'I must admit that I didn't think you would be able to get all that evidence from the gun.' He sighed. 'With hindsight, I should have given it a good clean before you got there.' The detectives looked at each other, eyes wide, unable to fathom what was going through the man's mind. 'It was all supposed to be a bit of a laugh,' David said, shrugging. 'You must be able to see that we didn't mean any harm. I was aiming at her arm, but the sights must have been off a little bit. I wouldn't have aimed at her head on purpose.'

'It was all supposed to be a bit of a laugh?' Jane repeated. 'Is that your explanation why you decided to shoot a 12-year-old girl in the face. Because it was a bit of a laugh?'

'Yes. I was pissed off with her because of what she said in the kitchen. So, I went upstairs and told Heather what she had said. Heather was upset that she had been slagging her off and I suggested shooting a pellet at her for a joke.' David looked as if it was the most sensible thing he had ever said and that everybody should understand. 'Heather was a bit dubious at first, but I told her because she had a big coat on it would just be like a sting and it would teach her a lesson. She would never know who fired the pellet. It wasn't meant to have ended like this; it was just a bit of a laugh.'

'Forgive me if I don't see the funny side of it, David. I will be charging you with grievous bodily harm with intent, for now but I'm going to be taking legal advice on whether we can up the charge.'

'You're just doing that because you don't like me,' David said, folding his arms. 'I told the other guy who was representing me at the first interview that she had it in for me and I was right. This has been blown out of all proportion. There's no need to take it this far, it was just a joke that's gone wrong.'

'I think it's best if we leave it there for now,' Jane said, standing. 'We need to speak to Heather again. Once we have concluded that interview and heard what she has to say, we'll be speaking to you again. The drug squad want a word, so stay where you are.'

'Oh, bloody brilliant,' David said, rolling his eyes. 'How long are you going to be keeping me in here? I'm starving and I want to go home.'

'We'll sort you out with something to eat in an hour or so, but I wouldn't expect to be going home for a few years.'

David looked like he'd been slapped in the face as the detectives left the room and closed the door behind them.

Chapter 38. Lenny and Jo

IT WAS ALREADY DARK when Lenny got home that day and it felt much later than it was. Jo was still upstairs in her office, chatting away in an online meeting. He didn't know how she did it day after day, dealing with children in dire straits. It was a vocation and certainly not a career that just anybody could take. He had heard a lot of the cases over the years, especially since COVID, when working at home had become the norm. The people that worked in child protection and safeguarding were a special breed indeed.

He went into the kitchen and the aroma of beef stew filled the air. The slow cooker was the best thing that they had ever bought. It was a must for couples who both work full time. Stick the ingredients in the pot, throw in some stock cubes and away you go. He took out a bottle of red and looked at the label. It was a wine he had never tried before and had arrived in a case of 12, that he had bought online with a discount code. You can't beat a good discount code, especially when it comes to wine, he thought. He opened it with a corkscrew and poured it into a large glass. He sniffed it and rolled it around the glass. It smelt the same as every other glass of red wine he had ever tried. No matter how many articles he read about the merits of certain wines and how to distinguish between the good and the not so good, he couldn't taste any dramatic difference between one or another. His palate was not sophisticated enough to tell the difference. He knew what he liked and that was good enough.

'Are you on the wine already?' Jo asked. She walked over to him and gave him a hug and a kiss. Since the shooting, she appreciated his arrival home after work so much more. Life wasn't the mundane routine that it had been. They appreciated every hour of every day and their time together seemed to be so much more precious than it had before. They say you don't appreciate what you have until it's gone and it's true. Never a truer word has been spoken.

'Have you finished yet or are you still working?' Lenny asked.

'I'll be another half an hour or so. I am just reading through some parenting assessments, and they are a pain in the arse.'

'It's okay. Take your time. I've got some figures that I need to go over before I go and see the accountant next week. You know what he's like if I haven't got everything ready for him. He just sticks another zero on the bill.' Jo hugged him again. 'Do you want a glass of wine to take upstairs with you?'

'Stupid question.'

Lenny and Jo spent the rest of the night cuddled together on the settee. They watched two episodes of Master Chef on catch up and then put on a horror film which was poorly made, with terrible acting, but it made them jump a couple of times. They both had an early start the next day, so they were upstairs and in bed for 11:30. Lenny lay awake for a while as he listened to Jo's gentle snoring become louder as she slipped into a deep sleep. Once she started there would be no stopping her until she woke up in the morning. Lenny got out of bed and tiptoed next door to the spare room, and in the peace and quiet he was asleep in minutes.

Chapter 39. The Hitman

I n the clearing stands a boxer, and a fighter by his trade, and he carries the reminders, of every glove that laid him down, or cut him till he cried out...

LEWIS CASHMAN LOOKED at the windows of the house and they were in darkness. There was no sign of life inside. It was late, the witching hour, and it seemed an appropriate time to kill. He dropped over the fence and landed silently on the grass, then tiptoed to the path which led to the back door. The lock was a simple mortice, and it took him seconds to click the tumbler and open the door. It creaked open, the hinges groaning a little, but he didn't think it would wake up his target. He couldn't understand why anyone would agree to be a witness. It was a sure way of getting yourself killed. He had made a lot of money silencing people permanently.

Lewis made his way across the kitchen to the hallway. Watery yellow light filtered through the glass in the front door. He moved silently to the bottom of the stairs and looked up. The silhouette of a man with a machinegun stopped him in his tracks. He put his hand on his weapon.

'Don't touch that gun, Lewis,' a voice said from behind him. The lights came on. Armed police officers had their weapons trained on him.

'How did you know I would be here?' Lewis asked, frozen to the spot.

'You've been followed since you left Dublin. Rupert Stokes went into witness protection yesterday, but we figured you were heading this way.'

Lewis smiled, widely and looked around the hallway and staircase.

'How many of you do you think I can take with me?'

'Don't do it, Lewis.'

Lewis pulled his Glock. He was dead before he even heard the gunshot that killed him.

Chapter 40. The Brother

JERRY SAMSON APPROACHED the block of flats from the grassy area to the rear. He had staked out the flat and surmised that Frankie and his goons were serving up ket from the back window of a downstairs flat. It was a bedroom. He watched a young girl buying and then riding off on her bike. She was thirteen if she was a day. Fucking scumbags, he thought. His sister was looking at a long stretch because of Frankie Wills. Yes, she had a mind of her own, but she was easily influenced. Leading her astray was simplicity itself and Frankie had a track record for fucking up people's lives. It was time to pay the ferryman.

The bedroom window closed, and Jerry pulled up his hood and walked across the grass. It was fifty yards at most. He reached the flat and rapped on the glass with his knuckles. A young lad with acne opened the window and Jerry punched him in the throat. The lad fell backwards, grasping his windpipe, gasping for air. He landed on the bed, softening the noise of the fall.

Jerry was through the window in a second, closing it behind him.

'Make a sound and you're dead, understand me?'

The lad nodded, tears streaming down his face. A wheezing sound was coming from his mouth and blood trickled from the corner of his mouth. Jerry crept around the bed and opened the door to the living room. He peered through the gap. Frankie was dozing on the settee, a glass of something red in his hand. His chin was on his chest, eyes closed. A film was on, something with a lot of gunfire and swearing. Jerry slipped through the doorway and walked to where Frankie was sitting. He kicked his feet to wake him up. Frankie opened his eyes and squinted. He looked confused and slightly amused.

'Jerry Samson,' he said, yawning. 'Your sister isn't here, which is a shame, I could do with wanking off. She gives a good wank, your sister. How did you get in?'

Jerry took out a bowie knife and held it up. Frankie opened his mouth and shook his head. Jerry stuck the blade into the centre of his chest, feeling his sternum snap. Frankie's eyes widened and a gurgling sound came from his throat. Jerry leaned on the knife, driving it through his back into the settee. He twisted the blade and pulled it out before slicing his throat from ear to ear. Blood gushed from the wound, pouring down his chest in a crimson wave. The life went from his eyes and his body slumped.

Jerry took the knife and wiped the blood from it on Frankie's hair. He left through the bedroom window, ignoring the teenager cowering in the corner. It wouldn't help Carla get out of prison, but it would stop others from going down in the first place.

Chapter 41. Six Months Later

But if this ever changing' world, in which we live in, makes you give in and cry, say live and let die...

PHIL MOULT KNOCKED on the front door of the Norris home. Adrian Norris opened it and stepped back to let Phil in. He looked anxious.

'You must be Adrian,' Phil said, offering his hand. 'I've heard all about you from your children.'

'Big Phil is in the house!' Jacob shouted, skipping out of the kitchen. He high fived him and repeated his chant. 'Big Phil is in the house!'

Joan Norris was in the kitchen, cooking something which smelled like scouse. She waved and washed her hands.

'Do you want a coffee?' she asked.

'Yes please. Where is she?' Adrian pointed to the living room. Phil popped his head around the living room door. Hope was sitting on the armchair, the twins squashed in next to her. They smiled and waved. 'Hello, you.'

'Hello Phil,' they said in unison.

'How is being at home suiting you?' he asked. Hope shrugged and smiled. 'Like you've never been away, eh?'

'It's very different,' Hope said. 'But so much better.'

'It's well different, big Phil,' Jacob said, standing on the settee. 'My dad used to be in jail and my mum used to be here but now, my mum is in jail and my dad is here. It's well better.'

'Sometimes change is good,' Phil said. 'I'm going to have a chat in the kitchen with your nan and your dad. I'll come and talk to you guys in a minute, okay?'

'Big Phil is in the kitchen!' Jacob chanted.

'Stop saying that, Jacob, you knob,' Pru said.

'Shut your face,' Jacob said, pulling out his tongue.

'Some things never change,' Phil said, smiling. Joan and Adrian Norris smiled and nodded. 'You've done a good job with them, Joan,' he added. 'I'm so pleased we kept the family together, and now you're home, they have the best chance of keeping it that way.'

SAM HAD BEEN HOME FROM work for a few hours when there was a knock on his door. He paused the film he was watching and opened it. It was a nice surprise.

'Mary. It's so good to see you,' he said. 'Come in.'

'It's good to be back,' Mary said, using a stick to help her walk. 'The housing have done a good job on my flat. If you don't mind everything painted white,' she added. 'You would never know anyone was stabbed to death in there. They never got anyone for his murder. I don't think anyone is too bothered, to be honest.'

'What are you like?' Sam said, laughing. He closed the door behind her. 'Is everything sorted now?'

'Yes. I got all my money back and the insurance paid out on the stuff they damaged, new settee, new bed, kitchen appliances and best of all, an eighty-five-inch television.'

'Wow. I wish someone would cuckoo my flat,' Sam joked. 'Did they break your television?'

'No. But I put the mop through the screen before the insurance assessor got there. It was on its way out anyway,' Mary whispered.

'You are a little bugger,' Sam laughed. 'Good for you. I saw the police at yours earlier, everything okay?'

'They came to tell me Andrew Head was sent to a young offenders' prison yesterday. He's in the psychiatric unit because he keeps trying to kill himself,' Mary said. 'He got four years for the attack on me and demanding money with menaces.'

'I heard that the top boss, Gary Booth got twenty-five years for murdering his dad,' Sam said. 'Small world. I don't think anyone will miss him either.'

'He got in with the wrong crowd.'

'I feel so sorry for his mother,' Sam said. 'That poor woman has been through the mill and back again.'

'Bless her. How is Andy?'

'He's good. I spoke to him yesterday,' Sam said. 'He's bought a two-bedroom semi in the same street as his parents. They live on the Wirral and the schools are better for Lucy. She never settled after her ordeal. I wish him all the best. Good luck to him.'

Sam and Mary chatted all night, and they shared a Chinese and two bottles of white wine. It was just like the old days, except they had the scars to prove what a difficult time they had been through. The main thing was that they had come out the other side, stronger and with the experience that life had shown them. All they could do was move on and enjoy whatever time they had left together.

Sam cleared the plates and went to the window to close the blinds. Four teenagers dressed in black track suits were standing on the corner at the end of the street. A car approached, slowed down, a few words were said, and a fist full of notes was handed through the window in return for something that he couldn't see. They were too far away but not far enough away for his liking.

He looked over the road and saw Sandra standing in her front window, as she so often did. She had dark circles beneath her eyes and was probably half the weight she had been the year before. She was wasting away a little more, each time he saw her. What happened to her husband and her son was sucking the life force from her. Sam felt a tinge of guilt, but it was not as bad as it had been. He had come to terms with what he had done and knew he couldn't change it. He vowed to live each day the best way he knew how, and to look forward, not back. The past was the past and behind him, his future was before him and that was the direction, he would walk in.

The End